Antiques and Apparitions

Cielle Kenner

ISBN 978-0-9729335-2-0
ASIN B0CS14RZSC

This version of *Antiques and Apparitions* has been revised and expanded with new scenes, deeper character development, and even more magic and mystery.

Get free bonus content at ciellekenner.com.

Contents

Welcome

WELCOME TO ENCHANTED SPRINGS, where ghosts are friendly, magic is real, and time is anything but linear.

Marley Montgomery never expected her Saturn Return to throw her life into full-blown retrograde, but moving back to her quirky hometown of Enchanted Springs unlocks more than childhood nostalgia. She's about to inherit more than just family heirlooms—she's inheriting a legacy.

Now, with spirits as her allies, magic at her fingertips, and mysteries lurking around every corner, Marley must navigate a world where history isn't just something you study—it's something you live.

Presenting "Antiques and Apparitions"

When a routine photo shoot on a Miami beach captures an impossible image—a mysterious flapper in 1920s swimwear—Marley is drawn into a mystery that transcends time. When the past starts pushing through the veil, Marley will have to embrace her newfound abilities and uncover the truth. Because some ghosts aren't content to be forgotten—and some shadows are dying to step into the light.

Cast of Characters

Marley Montgomery: A professional photographer whose magical abilities are revealed during her Saturn Return.

Clara Montgomery: Marley's grandmother and owner of the Enchanted Oven bakery, located across the street from the Enchanted Antique Shop, and head of Enchanted Spring's Council of Guardians.

Sadie Arragon: Marley's best friend. History professor by day, spellcaster by night. From Salem, Massachusetts. Age 30.

Eleanor Somerville: time-traveling witch and former proprietor of the Enchanted Antique Shop; Marley's mentor; best friends with Clara Montgomery; discombobulated from years of time travel; frail, birdlike, silver hair. Age: 90.

Violet Serrano: The vivacious spirit of a 1920s flapper, now living her best Afterlife at the Enchanted Antique Shop. Eternally 29.

Twila: Violet's spectral Siamese kitten; an adorable nuisance.

Jack Edgewood: Enchanted Springs police detective and overall man of mystery.

Ivy Sheridan: Enchanted Springs real estate agent. One of Marley's former classmates and a lifelong friend.

Scarlett Linden: Manager of the Opal Hush wine bar and a friend of Marley's family.

Endora "Dora" Spencer (aka "Madame Endora"): A psychic and astrologer who provides insights into Marley's Saturn Return.

Minor Characters

Natalie Fairchild: Ivy Sheridan's assistant.

Kate Davis: Gram's assistant at the Enchanted Oven Bakery.

Guest Stars

Colette Rios: 1940s owner of the Springs Hotel.

Ricardo Rios: Colette's Cuban husband.

Natasha Blast: A 1940s barmaid at the Springs Hotel

Irwin Foster: A clerk at the Springs Hotel in 1945.

Ghosts of the Past

Abraham Montgomery: Marley's great-great-grandfather, one of Enchanted Springs' founders.

Martha Snow: First proprietor of the Enchanted Antique Shop, then known as the Enchanted Springs Mercantile.

Hettie Stillson: The prim and proper church lady who demanded certain moral standards for the nascent village.

Henry and Sarah Addison: Founders of Enchanted Springs.

Theodore and Elizabeth Stevens: Friends of the Addisons and owners of a world-famous hat factory.

Chapter 1

The Golden Hour

A T FIRST, I THOUGHT it was a glitch.

The Miami sunset spread across the sky in dramatic strokes of orange and pink, filtered by soft, golden light. I framed the curve of the shoreline through my camera lens, ready to capture the waves catching the last glow of the day. My finger hovered over the shutter. And then—there she was.

A woman in the 1920s bathing suit.

She hadn't been there a second ago. I was sure of it. One minute, my lens was filled with a scenic panorama of the beach; the next, she was standing dead center in the frame.

She looked young and beautiful, but not in a way that fit the Miami vibe. No Brazilian bikini, no sunkissed balayage extensions. Instead, she wore a baggy, vintage-style swimsuit—a little tennis dress masquerading as beachwear. Her sleek bob framed a face that seemed both amused and mischievous, as if she'd just pulled off a harmless prank and I was the only one who'd noticed.

I wondered if it was all part of an elaborate practical joke—but practical jokes didn't usually come with the sound of distant jazz drifting on the breeze, or the unmistakable scent of lavender.

I blinked and lowered my camera, scanning the beach. She was nowhere to be seen. The shoreline was as empty as before, the sand dotted only by distant joggers and a scattering of seagulls.

Maybe it was a trick of the light. Or a reflection. Miami has its fair share of illusions—glamorous and otherwise.

But when I raised the camera again, there she was.

This time, she was posing. One hand rested on her hip, the other extended like she was balancing an invisible tray, her chin tilted up in a jaunty, theatrical angle. Her conspiratorial smile deepened, as though we were sharing a joke only she found funny.

Okay, I'd seen attention-seekers before, but this was next-level. Annoyed, I panned left. She followed. I panned right. She was there, winking, her face lighting up the frame no matter where I pointed the camera.

"Focus, Marley," I whispered to myself, though my heart was racing now, faster than any client deadline ever warranted.

I couldn't believe this was happening again.

For weeks now, I'd been brushing off strange little moments—dreams that felt too real, glimpses of shadows where none should be, flickers of something impossible in the corner of my eye. I'd blamed it on stress. Overwork. Too many late nights chasing the perfect shot.

But this? This was harder to dismiss.

I adjusted my grip on the camera and tried again, forcing myself to ignore the cold prickle running down my spine. The sunset wasn't going to wait for me to sort out my sanity. But as I steadied the frame, she appeared once more, closer this time, her dark eyes glinting with something unreadable. She was practically within arm's reach.

I yelped and dropped the camera to my side, my pulse thrumming in my ears. When I looked again, she was gone.

"Yoo hoo!"

The sing-song voice made me jump. I craned my neck, following the sound to the lifeguard stand.

She was perched high above me, chewing gum and kicking her legs like a kid on a playground swing. Her smile widened, toothy and bright. "Well, aren't you the cat's pajamas? All that posing on my part and not even a thank you for my time and trouble. Rude, don't you think?"

I froze, my brain scrambling for an explanation. "What are you doing up there?"

She blew a bubble with her gum, then popped it with her finger. "That's hardly important, is it? What matters is how you've been photographing me. What look are you going for? Dramatic? Playful? Or"—she leaned forward, a wicked gleam in her eye—"candid?"

"I didn't ask you to pose," I stammered.

"Oh, please." She flipped a hand in mock dismissal. "I'm a natural. You're lucky I graced your little photoshoot." She adjusted the bow on her swimsuit and struck another pose, this time with her hands clasped over her heart. "Do I look ethereal enough, or should I aim for something more grounded?"

Before I could respond, she jumped gracefully from the lifeguard stand, landing in a soft swirl of sand. For a moment, I thought I saw tiny stars shimmering around her... and then she vanished. Again.

I stood there, dumbfounded, the camera hanging limp at my side. The beach was empty now, save for the quiet waves rolling onto the shore.

"Okay," I whispered, slinging the camera over my shoulder. "That's enough strangeness for one day."

By the time I reached my Volkswagen convertible, the golden hour had slipped into twilight and the sky was a dusky blue. The world felt unnaturally still, like the hush before a storm. Even the familiar sounds of the beach—waves, seagulls, distant laughter—seemed muffled.

I drove in silence, trying to shake the weirdness, but the feeling followed me like a shadow. And that's when the signs started changing.

A billboard for Lucky Strike cigarettes caught my attention, with a healthful recommendation: "Reach for a smoke instead of a sweet." I snorted, figuring it was some sort of public service ad. Then I saw another one, this time for a new Charlie Chaplin movie. Beside it, the Ford Motor Company boasted about its "affordable" Model T. By the time I passed an announcement for the grand opening of the Biltmore Hotel, my fingers tightened on the steering wheel.

The Biltmore had been a Miami landmark for decades. How could it be having a grand opening?

My chest tightened.

Maybe it was some retro-themed marketing campaign, I told myself. Or maybe I'd just been working too much, with too little sleep and not enough food. That could explain it, right?

Chapter 2

Time Slips

B Y THE TIME I got home, my hands were trembling. I hadn't eaten all day, and my stomach was growling loud enough to audition for a monster movie. I dropped my camera gear on the counter, dug a beef burrito out of the freezer, and offered it as a peace offering to my low blood sugar.

As the microwave began its mystical hum—the closest thing to alchemy my kitchen could manage—I leaned against the cool granite countertop and stared out the floor-to-ceiling window at the Miami skyline.

The city stretched out before me, a glittering mosaic of lights, the high-rises punctuated by blinking red aircraft beacons. The ocean shimmered faintly in the distance, a soft reflection of the city's glow.

Usually, this view calmed me. Tonight, it felt distant, like I was staring at a postcard of a place I used to know.

I scarfed down the burrito in record time, the taste barely registering, and opened my laptop. The screen flickered to life, bathing the room in its pale glow as I slotted the memory card into the reader. My heart thudded in my chest, loud and insistent, as I clicked through the day's photos.

The first few images looked normal—waves, sand, the kaleidoscope of twilight on water. But then I saw that woman again, clear as day, staring directly at me in a shot I'd swear was empty when I snapped it. Her figure was impossibly sharp, as if she'd been the focus of the shot all along. Her eyes glinted with mirth. I could practically hear her laughter coming from the image.

I kept scrolling, my stomach twisting tighter with every click. She wasn't just in one photo—she was in dozens, each one sharper and clearer than the last. It was almost as if she'd been posing for me the entire time.

I leaned back in my chair, my breath caught somewhere between disbelief and panic. The air in the room seemed heavier now, charged with tension and a hint of danger.

I felt a faint vibration beneath my feet, like the building was shuddering in protest. The floor buckled and dropped, leaving my stomach in freefall. The world around me wobbled like a mirage, the edges of my vision blurring.

The walls began to dissolve, their sleek paint replaced by faded wallpaper in a bold floral pattern. My leather sofa melted away, replaced by a curvy turquoise couch with chrome legs, its upholstery worn but vibrant. A wooden record player appeared in the corner, its brass needle spinning over a vinyl record that hadn't existed a second ago.

A man sat on the sofa. He wore a slim-cut gray suit, his hair slicked back with almost obsessive precision. In one hand, he held a cocktail glass; the other tapped out a rhythm on his knee, perfectly in time with the faint music drifting through the air—a jaunty swing tune that felt utterly out of place in this century.

He didn't look at me. He didn't even seem to know I was there.

I blinked hard, my heart hammering as my sleek Scandinavian furniture morphed into mid-century modern designs. My LED lights flickered and died, their cold glow replaced by the warm hum of incandescent bulbs. My laptop vanished, replaced by a bulky black typewriter. Its keys gleamed under the light, like they were daring me to sit down and start typing.

The air smelled different now—faintly smoky, with a floral undertone I couldn't quite place. Perfume? Potpourri? I caught the muted clink of glasses and the low hum of conversation, as if a party were happening just beyond my reach.

I felt utterly displaced, as if I'd fallen through some invisible crack into another life entirely.

And then, just as quickly, it was over.

The music stopped. The record player disappeared. The man on the couch faded into nothing, and my apartment snapped back into sharp, modern focus. My leather sofa. My desk. My laptop, still open to the folder of photos.

My phone's cheerful ringtone shattered the silence, pulling me back to the present with a jarring finality. My hands shook as I grabbed it from the counter, swiping to answer.

"Hey, Gram," I said, my voice unsteady.

"Marley, dear!" She always sounded like she was smiling, and I could picture her now: flour dusting her apron, a spatula in one hand, the scent of cinnamon and vanilla filling her bakery. "How are you, sweetheart?"

I took a deep breath and forced a smile. "I'm good. How are you?"

"Have you eaten? I know how you get when you skip meals. Cranky and scatterbrained like your mother used to get, too."

I laughed. "Yes. I just finished a frozen burrito. I mean, it's not gourmet, but it's good enough."

A soft laugh floated through the receiver. "You always did have a soft spot for quick fixes. Now, I don't want to keep you, but I was hoping you could come home for the Founders Festival."

The words tugged at old memories—parades down Main Street, stalls lined with baked goods and crafts, the whole town buzzing with excitement.

"It's this weekend," she continued. "I know it's short notice, but Eleanor is hoping to make it her last hurrah before she retires. She's been at the antique shop for fifty years now, and she wants this festival to be something special. I thought it might be wonderful if you came home to take photos—capture those final moments of her legacy."

I leaned against the counter, her words stirring up a swirl of emotions. "Eleanor's retiring? I didn't think she would ever leave that shop."

"Neither did I," Clara admitted, her tone softening. "But she's ready. I think she wants to make this festival her grand send-off."

Eleanor had been a fixture of Enchanted Springs for as long as I could remember. Her antique shop wasn't just a business; it was part of the town's identity. Nestled on the corner of Main and Enchanted Avenue, its brick walls and creaky wooden floors held decades of history.

It also stood directly across the street from my grandmother's bakery, and the two of them—Eleanor and Clara—were best friends. They popped into each other's shops so often that it was never a surprise to find them in either place.

"She really wants you to take the photos," Gram said, her voice gently coaxing. "She says you have a gift for capturing moments."

I glanced at my computer screen, the folder of photos still open. The flapper's face stared back at me, her grin frozen in time. It was unnerving, that image—bright, sharp, and completely unexplainable. But the idea of going home, stepping away from whatever weirdness had settled around me, felt like a lifeline.

I thought back to the strange billboard ads, the flickering visions in my apartment, and the way my mind seemed to be playing tricks on me lately. A part of me was desperate to escape it all, to retreat somewhere familiar and safe.

"You know what, Gram? I think I could use a break. I'd love to come home."

There was a pause, and I could imagine my grandmother nodding in satisfaction. "I thought you might, dear. We'll be so happy to have you back. Safe travels, Marley. See you soon."

Chapter 3

Signs of the Times

THE NEXT MORNING, I was on I-4 heading north, leaving Miami and its shimmering skyline behind. The city faded in my rearview mirror like the closing credits of a movie, the bright lights of South Beach giving way to the flat, open countryside of Central Florida.

Gram's call had come at just the right time. Miami was wild and wonderful, sure—but lately, my life had felt like a surrealist painting, the edges of reality melting into something unrecognizable. The weirdness had been building, and I couldn't shake the feeling that it was all leading to something even stranger.

Like the other day, for instance.

I was on my way to meet a client about shooting some marketing photos for their newest real estate listing—a penthouse with enough marble and chrome to make Gatsby jealous. The sun was high in the sky, shining brightly, and I'd chosen a breezy halter dress that was as stylish as it was practical for Miami's heat. The streets buzzed with the rhythm of the lunchtime crowd.

And then, like a camera shutter snapping shut, everything changed. I blinked, and suddenly, it was night.

A full moon hung in the sky, silver light filtering through the swaying fronds of palm trees. The bustling business crowd was gone, replaced by clusters of people strolling leisurely, their voices soft and distant. I looked around, disoriented, trying to get my bearings.

The buildings were still there, but they weren't quite right. Their sleek glass facades had been replaced by the rounded edges and pastel hues of Art Deco architecture. Neon signs hummed and buzzed above me, their glow painting the sidewalk in shades of pink and blue.

Music drifted through the air, a lively jazz tune that made my heart skip a beat.

Ahead of me, a sleek building caught my eye. Its rounded corners gleamed under the moonlight, and the neon sign above the door announced The Flamingo Club. The sounds of swing music and laughter spilled onto the street, mingling with the faint scent of cigarette smoke and a hint of something floral.

I froze, staring at the open doors.

I should've turned around right then. Gone back to my modern world with its smartphones and office towers. But something pulled me forward. A tug of curiosity—or madness—propelled me inside.

The first thing I noticed was the smoke. It hung in the air like a ghost, swirling under the dim lights. My eyes adjusted, taking in the packed dance floor and the swirling colors of the room. People were dancing, spinning, moving with a rhythm that made my toes tap despite myself.

The women wore glamorous gowns with sequins that caught the light, their hair styled in sleek waves or soft curls. The men were sharp in tailored suits, their ties loose as they swayed to the beat of the music.

A jazz band played on a small stage, their instruments gleaming under the spotlights. The music was infectious.

I hesitated near the door, trying to stay out of the way as couples twirled past me. A man bumped into me—tall, handsome, and dressed like he'd just stepped off the set of a 1940s movie.

"Pardon me," he said. He gazed at me, then smiled.

"Would you care to dance?"

His suit was impeccably tailored, dark blue with subtle pinstripes that caught the light. A crisp white shirt and narrow black tie completed the look, and his slicked-back hair gleamed like polished obsidian.

His smile was charming, his eyes warm and mischievous. "I promise not to step on your toes."

My heart thudded in my chest. I didn't belong here. But then again, maybe I did—just for a moment.

"Well…" My voice faltered, but his confidence was contagious. He reached for my hand, and the warmth of his touch grounded me in this strange, impossible moment. "Sure."

He led me to the dance floor, the music wrapping around us as the crowd parted, moving aside like it had all been choreographed.

We moved together effortlessly, his hand firm but gentle on my waist as he guided me through the rhythm of the song. The world seemed to blur at the edges, leaving only the music, the laughter, and the glint of light on sequins and polished shoes.

I laughed as he twirled me again, the sound spilling out of me unbidden. If this was a dream, I didn't want to wake up.

As the music slowed, he released my hand and took a small step back. A wry smile flickered across his face. "Enjoy the moment," he said with a slight bow.

And then he was gone, melting into the crowd as if he'd never been there at all. The music faded, the room blurred, and I found myself back on the sidewalk, my camera bag still on my shoulder, and the sun shining overhead.

That was just the start.

A few days later, I stepped into my favorite coffee shop, already daydreaming about my next assignment and the promise of my usual latte with a dash of cinnamon. The air buzzed with the familiar sounds of baristas working their magic—steam hissing, beans grinding, and the clink of ceramic mugs hitting counters. The intoxicating smell of coffee enveloped me, and I couldn't help but smile.

The place was alive with energy. Cozy chairs and tables filled the space, while the walls showcased an eclectic mix of artwork by local artists—abstract splashes of color, moody portraits, and a few quirky prints that seemed like they were trying too hard to be ironic.

As I waited in line, my eyes drifted to a group of hipsters huddled around a table. Laptops glowed in front of them, their faces solemn as they sipped their meticulously crafted pour-overs. I adjusted the strap of my camera bag and shifted my weight, feeling a little out of place. Sure, I loved the vibe here, but I wasn't the type to get misty-eyed over single-origin beans or debate the merits of oat milk versus almond.

Then everything shifted.

It started as a subtle ripple. The air around me seemed to shimmer and fold, and suddenly, the familiar hum of the coffee shop disappeared.

When my vision cleared, I wasn't standing in line for a latte anymore. My heart thudded as I looked around. The coffee shop—my coffee shop—had disappeared, and I was standing in a gleaming, retro grocery store.

The rich aroma of coffee was gone, replaced by the faint smell of waxed linoleum and the tang of canned goods. The cozy tables and modern art had vanished, replaced by rows of metal shelves stocked with boxes of cereal and neatly stacked cans of soup.

I turned toward the window, half expecting to see a completely different cityscape, but the street outside was the same—almost. The buildings were still there, but the cars parked along the curb had fins and chrome bumpers that gleamed in the sunlight.

Around me, women shoppers wore bright, cheerful clothes that screamed 1960s suburbia—floral dresses with cinched waists or capris paired with sleeveless tops. Their hair was coiffed in perfect bouffants, some pinned with scarves, others rolled in pink curlers like they were ready for a beauty contest.

The sound of a radio crackled from somewhere overhead, playing a brassy rendition of "The Girl from Ipanema." A man behind the counter stood with a friendly smile, ringing up a woman's purchase on a clunky cash register.

I turned in a slow circle, trying to process the scene. Housewives strolled through the aisles with their carts, their heels clicking against the floor in a rhythmic melody. I caught flashes of old product packaging—Cheerios in simple yellow boxes, Jell-O in bold, primary colors, and cans of Green Giant vegetables. On one shelf, I spotted Tang and Bosco chocolate syrup, products I hadn't seen in decades, outside of retro commercials on YouTube.

No one noticed me.

In fact, one of the housewives walked right through me, her cart loaded with canned pineapple, tuna, and a brick of cream cheese.

My breath hitched as the cool sensation rippled through me, like the whoosh of air when a subway train barrels into a station. She didn't pause, didn't even shiver.

I was invisible. They were real—tangible, solid—and I was the ghost.

The surreal realization hit me like a slap, but before I could make sense of it, the world shifted again.

The grocery store vanished, the sound of the radio fading into the hiss of a steaming espresso machine. I was back in the coffee shop, the hum of modern life pressing in on all sides.

"Marley?"

I startled, spinning to see the barista staring at me with raised eyebrows. "Do you want your usual?"

I opened my mouth, but for a moment, no words came out. My fingers clutched my camera bag like it was a lifeline, my heart still racing.

"Yeah," I said finally, my voice steadier than I felt. "My usual."

She nodded and turned to make my drink, leaving me standing there, wondering if I was losing my mind—or if the world was trying to tell me something I wasn't ready to hear.

Chapter 4

Everything Old Is New Again

BEFORE I KNEW IT, I was back in Enchanted Springs.

For years, I'd thought of my hometown as little more than a sleepy speck on the map. But now, with each mile, I found myself anticipating the familiar sights and sounds of my childhood, as if some invisible thread was pulling me back.

Enchanted Springs couldn't have been more different from South Florida. While the two communities were just four hours apart in terms of travel time, they were worlds apart in mood and atmosphere. Miami, for example, was white sand and beaches; Enchanted Springs was tall trees and forests. Miami was high fashion and stilettos; Enchanted Springs was t-shirts and sneakers. Miami was late nights and bright lights, five-star dining and dancing 'til dawn. Enchanted Springs was up at dawn, rising with the sun to a cacophony of birdsong.

As I turned off the main highway and onto the scenic two-lane road that led to town, the pace of life seemed to slow. Spanish moss draped from the massive oaks lining the road, their branches forming a canopy overhead. A hawk circled lazily above, its sharp cry piercing the stillness. Wildflowers bloomed in bursts of color along the roadside, swaying gently in the warm breeze.

For decades, Enchanted Springs had been Central Florida's best-kept secret, a storybook village nestled in a bend of the river. Growing up, I'd found it hopelessly dull—a place where nothing ever happened, where I'd dreamed of escape. But as I approached the outskirts of our small town, I began to see it differently.

The streets were quieter here, the neighborhoods lined with tidy houses and manicured lawns that looked as well-maintained as ever. But downtown was different. Main Street, once a sleepy stretch of brick storefronts, had come alive.

The sidewalks were bustling with people—visitors snapping photos of vintage streetlamps, couples strolling hand in hand, families browsing the shops. Restaurants and cafés spilled out onto the sidewalks, colorful umbrellas shading patrons as they sipped iced tea or nibbled on fresh-baked pastries.

Even the storefronts, once hopelessly dated and frozen in time, seemed to have embraced their old-fashioned charm. A boutique clothing store showed off retro-inspired dresses in its window, while an old-fashioned candy shop lured customers with glass jars brimming with peppermints and taffy.

I slowed the car, taking it all in.

The town square was strung with fairy lights, already glowing faintly in the late afternoon sun. Signs for the upcoming

Founders Festival were everywhere, the bold lettering flanked by illustrations of cornucopias and ivy garlands. The festival had always been a cornerstone of Enchanted Springs, a celebration of its history and community—but now, it seemed bigger than ever.

From a marketing perspective, I was impressed. The banners looked like old-fashioned cabinet photos, featuring sepia-toned portraits of the city's founders.

I recognized Henry Addison, the white-bearded entrepreneur who founded our town, hoping to build a community of like-minded intellectuals. He seemed bright-eyed, even if he was a little bushy.

I spotted Hettie Stillson, the prim and proper church lady who demanded certain moral standards for the nascent village. In her portrait, she had her hair pulled into a tight bun, and her pursed lips expressed her perpetual disapproval.

There was Theodore Stevens, the world-famous hatmaker, sporting a trim mustache and goatee.

And then, much to my surprise, I saw a photo of my own great-great-grandfather, Abraham Montgomery.

His face caught me off guard. Unlike the others, his gaze seemed alive, piercing through the years with unsettling clarity. It felt like he wasn't just looking at the bustling modern-day streets of Enchanted Springs—he was looking into the future.

And why wouldn't he want to take a look? There was plenty to see. My old hometown was alive with movement, its sidewalks filled with people shopping, strolling, and sipping cold drinks.

The sweet scent of waffle cones drifted from the ice cream parlor, mingling with the perfume of flowers spilling from oversized planters that lined the street. Beneath the shade of colorful awnings, families rested on park benches, chatting and laughing as they watched the world go by.

Some people were already leaning into the festival's historical theme. Wherever I looked, costumed reenactors milled about as if they'd stepped straight out of another time, even though the festival was still several days away.

Near Penny's Candy Shop, a woman in a long calico dress adjusted the strings of her bonnet, her fingers deft and deliberate. Down by the hardware store, a Union soldier in a navy-blue Civil War uniform wiped his brow with a handkerchief that looked appropriately grimy. Outside the corner drugstore, two teenage girls in poodle skirts and saddle shoes giggled, heads bent together in a whisper.

It all felt oddly seamless, as if the town itself had conspired to create a living diorama of its history. Maybe it was the buildings—the two-story brick facades that stood proud and unchanging, their colorful awnings casting neat stripes of shade across the sidewalks. Or maybe it was the little touches: the Edison lightbulbs strung across the street, their soft glow already visible against the late-afternoon sun, or the American flags fluttering from the wrought-iron lampposts.

Whatever it was, I couldn't shake the feeling that Enchanted Springs wasn't just celebrating its history. It was living it.

Chapter 5

Ripples in Time

M Y GREAT-GREAT-GRANDPARENTS HAD BEEN drawn to
Enchanted Springs by the promise of Lincoln's Home-
stead Act. They'd planted citrus trees, then sold the grove when
it became too much to manage. Luckily, they kept the family
home on Stevens Street. That house had stood through decades
of storms and changes, its sturdy walls sheltering generations of
Montgomerys.

I let the thought settle over me, imagining my great-great-grandparents walking these same streets, when a sudden motion ahead
snapped me back to the present.

An old man in a rickety mule cart appeared out of nowhere, the
wooden wheels creaking as he jolted into view.

My heart leapt, and I slammed the brakes.

The old man was dressed like he'd stepped out of an antique photograph: a loose-fitting shirt with rolled-up sleeves, suspenders
holding up dusty trousers, and a straw hat shading his face. When

he turned toward me, I caught a fleeting glimpse of his features—hollow cheeks, a faint, polite smile, and eyes that seemed too dim, too faded, like the edges of an overexposed image.

He tipped his hat in a slow, deliberate gesture, nodding at me as if to say, "Pardon the intrusion."

The mule plodded forward with unhurried grace, its shaggy coat swaying with each step. Its downturned ears twitched faintly, oblivious to the modern world it had wandered into. The heavy clop of its hooves against the brick road rang out impossibly clear, cutting through the hum of my car engine and the faint chatter of the town beyond my windshield.

The scene in front of me softened at the edges, like light refracted through a haze of heat. The air shimmered, and for a moment, the colors of the world seemed to dull—the bright reds of the awnings muted to rust, the green of the trees fading to sepia tones.

I watched, frozen, as the mule cart crossed the sunlit street. The man's figure grew fainter with each step, blurring at the edges like a mirage dissolving in the light.

Then, just as abruptly as they'd appeared, they melted into the shadowy mouth of a narrow alley. The clatter of the cart wheels faded, swallowed by the darkness.

I sat there, hands gripping the steering wheel, my breath shallow. The air inside the car felt too thick, heavy with the weight of something I couldn't name.

What had I just witnessed?

I blinked, half-expecting to spot the cart lingering in the alley. But there was nothing—just a dark, empty space where they had vanished without a trace.

A nervous laugh escaped my lips, startling me in the quiet. "You're imagining things, Marley," I muttered, the sound of my own voice grounding me.

First the flapper, now this?

I shook my head, trying to dispel the unease crawling along my skin. I needed to get a grip. Or a very strong drink.

I drove a little farther and the Springs Hotel came into view, its Spanish Revival façade glowing softly in the muted light.

I'd passed the building thousands of times growing up, but I'd never really noticed it. Today, its white stucco walls and arched doorway seemed to radiate a quiet allure, as if the building itself were finally demanding to be seen.

I pulled my car into a space along the curb, grabbing my camera bag from the back seat. Framing the hotel in my viewfinder, I adjusted the settings. The wrought-iron streetlamps stood like sentinels, their intricate curves adding contrast to the timeless structure. A low bank of clouds diffused the sunlight, softening the shadows and creating the perfect conditions for the shot.

I stepped back, studying the building from a distance. The stucco walls and red-tiled roof were pristine, the arched windows hinting at its storied past. For the first time, I wondered why I'd never stopped to admire it before.

I clicked the shutter, and the camera's familiar whir grounded me in the moment.

The sun hung high in the sky, the Florida heat pressing against my skin. The idea of stepping inside for a drink felt too tempting to resist. Slinging the camera strap over my shoulder, I pushed open the double doors and crossed the threshold into another world.

Inside, the lobby had been transformed into the Opal Hush wine bar, a space that blended old-world charm with modern sophistication. Velvet sofas and leather armchairs formed intimate clusters, their jewel tones glowing under the warm light of pendant fixtures. The original check-in desk had been reimagined as a sleek bar, its polished wood and brass accents paying homage to the past.

The light shifted a bit, and I thought a cloud had passed overhead—but the change was deeper, stranger. The air around me seemed to thicken, the wine bar fading like a dream slipping through my fingers.

The soft glow of the pendant lights dimmed, replaced by the sepia tones of another time. The polished floor gleamed faintly in the warm light of a grand chandelier, its crystals catching the muted rays like tiny stars.

I blinked, my breath catching as the modern decor peeled away, replaced by the Springs Hotel lobby as it must have looked in the 1940s.

The scent of leather and cedar gave way to lemon-scented furniture polish, a hint of tobacco smoke, and perfume. Women in fitted dresses glided through the space, their heels clicking softly against the tiled floor. Men in suits lingered near the check-in desk, the shine of their Oxfords catching the light as they exchanged quiet words.

Behind the desk stood a short, balding clerk, adjusting his thick-framed glasses with quick, fidgeting movements. He glanced around the room nervously, as though waiting for something—or someone.

Across the lobby, a redheaded woman swept into view. She carried a manila folder in one hand, her fitted suit and string of pearls emphasizing her hourglass silhouette. A ruby brooch sparkled on her lapel.

Her movements were deliberate, her gaze sweeping the room with an intensity that made me hesitate.

Instinctively, I raised my camera. The click of the shutter sounded loud—too loud—but no one else seemed to notice. No one, except her.

The redhead froze, her eyes locking onto mine. Her lips parted as if to speak, but no sound came.

I blinked, and she was gone.

The sepia tones dissolved. The hum of the wine bar rushed back in like a tide, the warmth of the modern decor settling around me once more.

I froze, my breath shallow, as if the very air had been pulled from my lungs. Slowly, I lowered my camera and reviewed the image on the screen.

There she was—the redhead. Frozen mid-step, her face sharp and vivid, her piercing gaze locked on mine.

My hands trembled as I stared at the photo. I think part of me had hoped that heading home would put an end to the strange time shifts I'd experienced in Miami.

Clearly, that wasn't the case. I turned on my heel and headed back out to the street.

Chapter 6

Sugar, Spice, and Sentiment

M Y GRANDMOTHER'S BAKERY WAS just three blocks away. I drove there, pulled into a parking spot right out front, and let the familiar scent of fresh-baked bread and sugary confections wash over me. It wafted through the air, mingling with the faint tang of citrus from the planters lining the sidewalk.

The building looked just as it always had, with its pastel-painted façade and whimsical lettering that spelled out "The Enchanted Oven." The sight of it made something inside me unclench, a tether pulling me back to solid ground. After weeks that felt like the universe had pressed fast-forward and rewind at random, this place was a welcome anchor to reality.

I grabbed my bag and headed inside. The bell above the door jingled softly, its cheery chime greeting me like an old friend. Warmth enveloped me, along with the rich scent of cinnamon and vanilla. Sunlight streamed through the windows, casting golden patches across the wooden floor, and for the first time in days, I felt the tightness in my chest begin to ease.

For now, at least, I was home.

I took a deep breath, letting the scent of cinnamon and sugar wrap around me like a favorite blanket.

Through the large front windows, I could see rows of treats displayed on gleaming glass shelves. Cookies dusted with sparkling sugar, brownies crowned with glossy ganache, and Gram's famous citrus muffins with their golden tops dotted with flecks of zest all called to passersby, daring them to resist. Each tray was a tiny masterpiece, so perfect it made me want to press my face to the glass, just like I'd done as a kid.

I could see into the kitchen, where Gram stood at her worktable, her hands moving deftly as she crimped the edges of a pie crust. Flour dusted her apron and smudged her cheek, a telltale mark of someone who worked magic in the kitchen.

Her eyes lit up when she saw me. "Marley!" she exclaimed, dusting her hands on her apron and hurrying toward me.

Her dimples framed her radiant smile, and laugh lines crinkled at the corners of her eyes as she wrapped me in a tight embrace.

"Hey, Gram," I said, my voice muffled against her shoulder.

She pulled back just enough to get a good look at me, her hands resting lightly on my arms. "Well, aren't you a sight for sore eyes! It's been too long."

Gram had always been effortlessly beautiful, the kind of woman who could turn heads without even trying. Her auburn hair, still free of grays thanks to her best friend Sharon and her salon magic, was twisted into a messy bun that somehow looked elegant. The dimples and laugh lines that framed her smile only added to her warmth, making her face as welcoming as the bakery itself. I know I resembled her, but I could only hope to age as gracefully as she had.

I looked around again, happy to find myself in familiar surroundings.

The Enchanted Oven had been my second home growing up, especially when my parents were off on one of their many archaeological digs or expeditions. Everything looked just as I remembered it.

Gingham curtains in cheerful shades of red and white framed the windows, fluttering slightly in the breeze from the ceiling fan overhead. The glass display case that doubled as a checkout counter was filled with pies—apple, cherry, peach—all perfectly golden, their fillings just beginning to peek out from their latticed crusts. Frosted cupcakes stood proudly beside tall layered cakes, while loaves of bread lined the wooden baker's rack behind the counter. Crisp baguettes nestled in wicker baskets, their crusts golden and inviting.

Gram guided me to one of the small bistro tables by the window, each one adorned with a simple bouquet of fresh daisies in a mason jar. Her assistant, Kate Davis, appeared moments later, a salted caramel brownie on a delicate floral dessert plate balanced in her hands.

"Welcome home," Kate said with a grin, setting the plate in front of me. Her blonde ponytail swung as she turned back toward the kitchen, where the soft chime of a timer signaled the arrival of another batch of brownies. Kate was about my age, though her easy familiarity with the bakery and her practiced movements spoke to the years she'd spent as Gram's trusted right hand.

While Kate headed back into the kitchen to pull more brownies out of the oven, Gram poured me a cup of coffee from a carafe on the counter.

I glanced out the window. Main Street was alive with activity. The sidewalks were bustling, and quite a few people were dressed in elaborate period costumes. A man in a navy-blue fedora and trench coat leaned casually against a lamppost, engrossed in his newspaper. Across the street, three women in polka-dot dresses with bright red lipstick laughed together, their gestures animated as if they'd just shared the juiciest gossip. Even their hairstyles—sleek victory rolls—were era-perfect.

"Looks like the town's really getting into the spirit of the weekend," I said, gesturing toward the street with my coffee cup.

Gram chuckled softly, her eyes twinkling with a hint of mischief. "Oh, my dear, you have no idea. There's more to it than just a celebration."

Her tone sent a shiver of anticipation through me, and for a brief moment, the cozy bakery felt strangely charged, as if the air was filling with a buildup of static electricity. The hum of the ceiling fan and the soft clatter of plates in the kitchen seemed distant, as though the air itself had shifted, carrying a faint, invisible current.

Out in front of the bakery, an elderly couple moved slowly past the bakery, their steps deliberate and careful. The old man leaned heavily on his cane, while his wife clasped his arm with a tenderness that spoke of decades shared. She murmured encouragement to him, her voice too soft for me to hear through the glass.

It would've been an ordinary enough sight, except for one strange detail: the woman seemed to be walking in a sunbeam that followed her, a golden glow that danced at her feet no matter where she moved.

"Gram," I said, my voice low, "look how the sun is shining on that woman."

She glanced out the window, her gaze softening as she recognized the couple. "Oh, that's Millicent and Ned Gardener. It's so nice to see them together again."

There was something about the way she said it, as if there was more meaning in her words than I could decipher.

Gram turned back to me and set her coffee cup down with deliberate care. Then she leaned across the table, her eyes narrowing slightly, her voice dropping to a near-whisper.

"Marley," she said, "have you noticed anything odd lately?"

Chapter 7

Eleanor Somerville

M Y GRANDMOTHER'S QUESTION HUNG in the air, charged and heavy, and my pulse quickened. My hand tightened around my coffee mug as if it could somehow ground me.

"No," I said reflexively, the word slipping out too quickly. I didn't want her to think I'd flipped my lid.

How could I even begin to explain the things I'd seen? The flapper at the beach, the grocery store that wasn't a grocery store, the redheaded woman caught in my camera? How could I explain the growing sense that the world around me was shifting, blurring, like an old photograph developing into something new—and yet impossibly old?

I couldn't. Not without sounding like I'd lost my grip on reality.

Before I could elaborate—or talk myself into admitting more—the door to the bakery swung open, and Eleanor

Somerville bustled in, bringing a gust of energy that swept through the room like a fresh breeze.

Eleanor was tiny but formidable, a birdlike woman with silver curls that refused to be tamed and a face lined with the kind of wisdom you earned through decades of living. Age hadn't dulled her sparkle, though—her pink lipstick and softly penciled brows framed a pair of eyes that twinkled with mischief. She wore rhinestone clip-on earrings and a string of graduated pearls, her outfit completed by a pale green cardigan with a single jeweled button at the collar.

Her gaze landed on me, and her face lit up with a genuine smile. "Marley, my dear, you're back!"

She navigated the café tables with practiced ease, her small frame moving lightly through the space. I stood as she approached, and she wrapped me in a hug that was surprisingly tight for a little old lady. She almost squeezed the air out of my lungs.

"We've been waiting for you," she said, pulling back just enough to study my face. Her sharp eyes held a mix of affection and something else—anticipation, perhaps?

"It's good to be back," I said, my smile coming easily under her warmth. "I've missed this place."

Eleanor patted my hand affectionately. "And this place has missed you, dear."

I sighed contentedly. Coffee, a brownie, and the comforting presence of Gram and Eleanor—I felt more grounded than I had in weeks.

Gram rose to get a a cup of tea for Eleanor, the porcelain clinking softly against the saucer as she set it down. "Tell Marley about the festival," she urged with a knowing smile.

Eleanor's face lit up, and she took a careful sip of tea before diving in. "Oh, there's going to be a bit of everything. A parade to kick things off, of course, and a band concert, plus tours of historic sites. And don't forget the old-fashioned baseball game, with players in proper period uniforms!"

Gram's tone brimmed with pride. "The craft show and farmer's market are happening in Courthouse Square," she added. "Booth spaces sold out months ago—it's going to be packed."

Eleanor nodded. "Everyone's encouraged to dress in period costumes, too. That's been great for business at the antique shop—we've sold everything from pioneer dresses to vintage suits."

"And the street dance under the stars," Gram said, her smile widening. "Don't forget about that. The fireworks show at the end will be the grand finale."

I could picture it all in my mind—the vibrant crowds, the sounds of laughter and music, the glow of festival lights strung through the trees. It sounded magical, the perfect mix of nostalgia and celebration.

"It sounds like this weekend is going to be one for the history books," I said, glancing at my camera bag. "I can't wait to capture it all. In fact, I'd kind of like to get a head start, and scout around for locations and lighting."

Gram's eyes sparkled with approval. "Why not start at Courthouse Square? They've just finished decorating around the World's Fair Fountain."

Eleanor smiled in agreement, her voice bright with encouragement. "I was about to suggest the same thing. It's beautiful right now."

I slung the camera bag over my shoulder, excitement humming through me. "Courthouse Square it is," I said. "I'll head over now."

With a wave and promises to catch up later, I stepped outside and into the sunlit streets of Enchanted Springs.

Chapter 8

The Courthouse

I TURNED WEST AT the corner, heading toward Court-house Square. The afternoon sun's warmth was tempered by a light breeze that carried the faint scent of fresh-cut grass and something floral—probably jasmine, unless someone had figured out how to bottle nostalgia and spray it across town.

If Courthouse Square was the centerpiece of Enchanted Springs, the courthouse itself was its crown jewel. Built over a century ago, the building had aged like a classic film star—maybe a few wrinkles here and there, but still commanding attention. Its copper rotunda, once gleaming, now sported a soft green patina. At its peak, the clock tower ticked steadily, its rhythmic hands like a heartbeat for the town.

I raised my camera, framing the scene in my viewfinder. The oak trees flanking the courthouse added a natural symmetry, their sprawling branches draped with Spanish moss that swayed in the breeze, catching the light like a sequined shawl. The courthouse looked alive, the moss and shadows playing across its surface like whispers from another time.

I adjusted the focus, waiting for the perfect moment when the clock's hands would align at the top of the hour. In that fleeting intersection of past, present, and future, the clock chimed and I clicked the shutter.

Perfect.

I moved closer, zeroing in on the details that told the courthouse's story. The brickwork was a patchwork of time—its weathered surface pocked and scarred, but stubbornly holding on. The courthouse door, its edges worn smooth and its brass hardware gleaming, begged for a close-up. Every scratch, scuff, and faded spot whispered of lives that had passed through, secrets that had been carried in and out, and stories that had begun or ended within its frame.

I crouched low, framing the intricate detailing of the brickwork, the craftsmanship of the windows, and the way the afternoon light danced off the glass.

Finally, I stepped back to capture the full panorama. The courthouse stood framed by its surroundings—the sprawling oaks, the dappled sunlight, and the blue sky above. The shot felt alive, the heart of Enchanted Springs beating strong and steady in every detail.

Across the street, Courthouse Square was bustling.

Townspeople strolled along the brick walkways, weaving past oak and magnolia trees. Near one entryway, a hot dog vendor adjusted the umbrella on his cart, while an ice-cream vendor at another offered scoops to a toddler with sticky hands and an unsteady grip on their cone.

Near me, a young mother pushed twins in a double stroller. Across the way, a teenager in a baseball cap whizzed past on a skateboard, earning a disapproving glance from a woman who clutched at her shopping bags. Over near the band shell, a cluster of junior-high students seemed to have commandeered the stage for an after-school rendezvous.

At the center of it all stood the World's Fair Fountain, its waters leaping and cascading in a mesmerizing display. This was no ordinary fountain—it was a relic of the 1939 New York World's Fair that had found its way back to town and been granted a place of honor. Even in the daylight, the fountain seemed to glow, its waters shimmering with an almost otherworldly phosphorescence. The colorful azaleas surrounding it only added to the effect, their blossoms a riot of pinks and reds that framed the scene like a living postcard.

Near the fountain, a trio of elderly women in floral dresses sat chatting, their parasols tilted just so to shield them from the sun. And there, near a shaded bench, a man dressed in what looked like a 1920s suit tipped his hat at a passing woman in a gingham dress. They exchanged pleasantries before disappearing into the crowd.

I raised my camera, adjusting the settings as I aimed at the fountain. The late-afternoon light played perfectly off the water's surface, and I knew this shot would capture not just the scene but the magic of Enchanted Springs. The azaleas made for a vibrant foreground, their petals catching the sunlight just enough to pop against the darker greens of the magnolias.

As I adjusted the focus, the lively hum of the square began to fade—not all at once, but slowly, like the volume on life itself was being turned down. A cool sharpness crept into the air, and goosebumps rose on my arms despite the warmth of the sun.

I hesitated, my finger hovering over the shutter as an odd prickle of unease tickled the back of my neck.

I glanced at my camera's display. Among the ordinary images of water and flowers, a figure emerged, as though stepping out from the folds of time itself.

At first, it was like watching an old filmstrip flicker into focus. A figure stepped into the frame, her movements smooth, her form sharp and vivid against the soft blur of the fountain's backdrop. She was draped in the unmistakable glamor of the 1920s—a flapper, her bobbed hair swinging, her dress a shimmer of sequins and fringe.

There was no mistaking her—it was the same bathing beauty I'd seen in Miami.

This time, though, she didn't pop in and out of sight. When I lowered the camera, she was still there, as radiant and tangible as the fountain itself. She practically glowed, her figure surrounded by a halo of soft, golden light that made her seem both ethereal and undeniably present.

"Welcome home, Toots!" she exclaimed. "Long time, no see!"

I stepped even closer. No one else seemed to see her, but at least she wasn't disappearing from view this time.

"Who are you?" I asked.

She smiled, tilted her head, and, with a mischievous glint in her eye, began dancing to a beat only she could hear. If I wasn't mistaken, she was doing the Charleston right there by the World's Fair Fountain. "I'm a dancer, dollface!"

With a playful bounce, she did a series of quick steps forward and backward. She kicked her legs and her arms swung in perfect opposition, adding balance and flair. She twirled and swiveled with an infectious joy, her fringed dress swirling around her. I couldn't help but laugh, the sound mingling with the soft splash of the fountain's waters.

When the impromptu dance ended, she bounced over to my side, leaning in to peer at my camera's screen. "Well, isn't this the bee's knees? You can see your Kodaks before they're even developed. Let's have a look, shall we? I want to see if time has been kind to this old gal."

I was confused. "What do you mean? Can't you see yourself?"

She threw her head back and laughed, the sound rich and carefree. "In a mirror? Sure. I'm a ghost, not a vampire. But can I see my luscious backside? Not in any form so far. That's the real tragedy."

I flipped through the images, each photo capturing her with striking clarity. In one shot, the sequins on her dress sparkled like diamonds; in another, her legs formed the perfect arc of a high kick. She nodded approvingly at each one.

"Oh, look at that! I always did have great gams. If I do say so myself, I've still got it," she exclaimed, pointing to a particularly striking pose where the light caught the sequins of her dress, making her shimmer against the backdrop of the fountain. "Not that I ever doubted."

Before I could ask another question, she twirled away, her laugh echoing as her figure dissolved into a burst of light and a flurry of tiny, shimmering stars. The fountain erupted in a sudden, dramatic geyser, water shooting high into the air before cascading down in a sparkling deluge that left me—and half the square—drenched.

I blinked, wiping water from my face as the world around me seemed to snap back to normal. The bustling noise of the square returned, the chill in the air lifted, and people resumed their conversations as though nothing had happened.

But I knew better. The dampness on my skin and the photos on my camera told a different story—one I wasn't sure anyone else would believe.

Chapter 9

The Saturn Return

A FTER THE STRANGE ENCOUNTER at Courthouse Square, I found myself heading back to the Enchanted Oven. The bakery's familiar warmth beckoned me, though my thoughts were anything but cozy.

The camera strap dug into my shoulder, the weight of the strange images it carried feeling heavier than it should.

When I pushed the door open, the brass bell chimed softly, and Gram looked up from the till, where she was counting cash with the precision of someone who had done it a million times.

Her eyebrows lifted in mild surprise. "What brings you back so soon? Don't tell me you've already run out of photos to take."

I managed a small smile, moving closer as I slid the camera off my shoulder. "Gram," I started, hesitating as my thumb hovered over the screen. I scrolled through the photos until I landed on her. "I saw something strange at the fountain."

Gram paused mid-count, her curiosity piqued.

Turning the camera around, I showed her the screen. Among the shots of cascading water and vibrant azaleas was the unmistakable figure of the flapper, shimmering like a memory brought to life.

"Do you recognize this woman?"

Gram leaned in, her eyes narrowing as she studied the image. Then, to my astonishment, she chuckled, her face lighting up with recognition. "Oh, I do," she said, her tone a mix of amusement and affection. "I'll tell you all about her as soon as I close up."

With practiced ease, she ushered out the last two customers of the day, her warm smile never faltering as she bid them goodnight. The bell above the door chimed softly with each departure. At five on the dot, Kate poked her head out from the kitchen to say a cheerful goodbye before slipping out the back door.

The bakery quieted, the usual background noise of the ovens and mixers replaced by a tranquil stillness that made the space feel almost expectant.

Gram locked the front door and gestured toward the corner of the bakery where two comfortable chairs sat facing each other. It was a spot we'd used for many family heart-to-hearts over the years, surrounded by the comforting scent of fresh bread and the faint hum of the refrigerators.

I followed her over, settling into the familiar chair as she lowered herself into the other, the weight of generations seeming to rest lightly on her shoulders.

"Marley," Gram began, her voice carrying that knowing tone that meant I was about to hear something big. "I knew you'd be back this weekend. I've known for months. After all, it's your Saturn Return."

"My what?"

"Your Saturn Return," she repeated, as though it were the most natural thing in the world. "Dora and I checked your transits."

I blinked. "Transits?"

"Your astrological transits," she explained, her expression brightening at the mention of her longtime friend. "You remember Madame Endora, don't you?"

I nodded. Of course, I remembered Madame Endora. She was one of Gram's best friends. She ran *Enchantments*, the town's go-to psychic parlor, where tourists could stop in for tarot readings and mystical charms.

"She's a very talented astrologer," Gram continued, leaning forward. "She charts the current movement of the planets and compares them to your birth chart. Fascinating work."

"So the stars told you I'd come back?" I tried to keep my tone light, but I probably sounded as bewildered as I felt.

Gram laughed softly. "Not exactly. The Saturn Return happens to everyone your age, but your chart shows something rare. Marley, you have gifts most people can only dream of."

I shrugged, trying to look nonchalant. "Like photography?"

"Oh, you're a brilliant photographer." She waved her hand as if that was a given. "But your abilities go far beyond that."

Her hands cupped mine, her warmth grounding me even as her words sent my thoughts spiraling.

"Marley, you're a Montgomery. And now that you've experienced your first Saturn Return, you've come into your birthright, your heritage, your gifts."

I tilted my head, skepticism edging into my tone. "What does that mean, exactly?"

Her smile widened, a glimmer of excitement in her expression. "It means your abilities are waking up, my dear."

Before I could respond, Gram gestured toward the camera in my lap. "And that woman you saw at the fountain—Violet Serrano—is part of it. She's what you might call a family friend. Normally, she keeps to the Enchanted Antique Shop, so seeing her out and about is quite something."

"She's not just at the shop. I saw her on the beach in Miami."

Gram nodded, entirely unfazed. "Violet does like to be where the action is. It's entirely possible she overheard Eleanor and me talking about you, so she popped down to see you for herself."

I leaned back, shaking my head. "I wish this made sense."

"It will," Gram said, her tone as warm and reassuring as the bakery itself. "You've reached a pivotal age, Marley. Our family has certain unique abilities that awaken during this time. Think of it as a supernatural coming of age."

She leaned forward, squeezing my hands with the conspiratorial air of someone about to spill the family's juiciest secret. "All Montgomery women have a gift. And now that you've experienced your Saturn Return, you've come into your birthright."

I blinked at her, my mind scrambling for a response. "Wait. My what now?"

"You have the ability to see beyond the veil of time," she explained, her voice steady. "Those people you've been seeing, like the costumed characters out on the street? They're not reenactors. They're ghosts. Spirits from the past. And you, my dear, are finally seeing them—because it's your legacy."

I pulled my hands back, crossing my arms as I leaned away from her. "That's funny. Really. Are we being recorded? Are you posting this online somewhere? Because if this is your version of a prank, it's not exactly your style."

"Marley, I'm serious."

I searched her face for a flicker of mischief, some hint that she was messing with me. But her expression stayed calm and sincere, her eyes full of quiet certainty.

A chill rippled down my spine. Ghosts? That couldn't be right. But deep down, a part of me—the part that had seen a flapper vanish into a burst of light and stars—knew it wasn't just a trick of the light or my imagination.

"So, you're saying these visions are real?" My voice sounded small, even to me. "It's not my brain short-circuiting or some weird sleep deprivation thing? I'm truly seeing spirits?"

"Yes." Her answer was simple, firm, and utterly inescapable.

I laughed, though the sound came out brittle. "That's not possible. I'm just a photographer, not a sorcerer."

Gram's gaze softened, her understanding cutting through my denial. "You can tell yourself that all you want, but the truth has a way of showing itself when you least expect it. You're part of a long line of powerful, magical women, and this town is tied to your destiny."

My mouth opened, then closed again. I stared at her, waiting for the punchline. When none came, I let out an exasperated groan and leaned back in my chair. "You're serious."

"I am," she said, reaching for my hand again. Her warmth steadied me, even as her words spun my world sideways. "I still remember what it was like when I came into my magic. It threw me for a loop, too. Of course, I was already married, and your mother was a toddler at the time, so I didn't exactly have the freedom you do now." She smiled wistfully, her expression tinged with both nostalgia and excitement. "I envy you a little. You get to explore your magic without those responsibilities."

I stared at her, the word magic ringing in my ears. It sounded ridiculous. Impossible. And yet, deep down, I felt the tug of something real—something that had always been there, just out of reach, waiting for me to notice.

"What if I don't want this gift?"

Her smile softened. "You might not want it now, but it's a part of you, Marley. It always has been. And when the time comes, I think you'll find it's more of a blessing than a burden."

I didn't answer. I wasn't sure I could.

Chapter 10

Sadie Arragon

A KNOCK AT THE door startled us, shattering the quiet spell that had settled over the bakery.

Gram glanced at the clock, then crossed the room with her usual brisk efficiency, unlocking the door and swinging it open. A cool evening breeze swept in, carrying the faint scent of night-blooming jasmine—and a woman I'd never seen before.

Her platinum blonde bob fell in a precise, clean line that framed her face perfectly, accentuating sharp cheekbones and a jawline that could probably cut glass. Her horn-rimmed glasses added an intellectual edge, though her green eyes held a glint of something playful. She wore a tailored blazer over a vintage-inspired blouse, paired with slim trousers and ankle boots. It was classic, with just enough modern flair to make it clear she wasn't trying too hard.

She stepped inside, her gaze immediately landing on me. "Ah, you must be Marley," she said, her voice warm and smooth, like a cup of tea on a rainy day. She extended a hand. "Sadie Arragon."

Gram closed the door and turned to me, smiling as she motioned for Sadie to sit. "Sadie is the new history professor Magnolia University. She's filling in for your mother while your parents are on sabbatical."

"Oh," I said, the pieces clicking into place. My parents had been professors at Magnolia University for as long as I could remember, and their sabbaticals were typically split between digging through archaeological sites and hunting for obscure texts in far-off libraries.

I shook Sadie's hand, caught off guard by her directness. "Nice to meet you, Professor Arragon."

"Please, call me Sadie. Everyone does."

Her eyes flicked to the photo displayed on my camera, still resting on the table. A spark of recognition brightened her expression, and she leaned closer. "That woman! She looks like an authentic flapper!"

I hesitated, unsure how much to say, but Gram didn't share my caution. She chuckled softly, her tone rich with amusement. "That's because she is a flapper."

Sadie's eyebrows shot up, but instead of questioning it, she smiled knowingly. "Interesting."

Gram gestured for Sadie to join us, pulling out a chair and motioning to the table. "Sadie is one of us, Marley," she said lightly, though her words carried a weight I couldn't quite ignore.

"One of us?" I repeated, glancing between them and half-expecting someone to laugh and say, Just kidding.

Sadie smirked, a glimmer of mischief in her eyes. "She means witches, Marley. Although I prefer 'spellcaster.' It's more precise."

"Right. Witches," I said dryly. "Next, you'll tell me there's a flying broomstick parked outside."

Sadie laughed, her head tilting back. "No. Just a Subaru."

I smiled. At least she had a sense of humor about this.

"I know it's a lot to take in. But that's why I came. Your grandmother said you'd be here soon, and I thought maybe you could use a friend."

She reached for a chair and setting her tote bag on the floor. "I've heard so much about you, I feel like we already know each other. I didn't realize how much you would look like Clara, though."

Gram beamed. "The Montgomery women are all cut from the same cloth, I'm afraid."

Sadie tilted her head, studying me for a moment before nodding. "I can see that. But you've got your own energy, too—sharp, creative. That'll serve you well."

I wasn't sure how to respond, but there was something undeniably likable about her. She was serious without being stuffy, and her stylish demeanor was balanced by an unassuming sweetness.

Her gaze drifted toward the refrigerated case. "I came by to meet you, of course, but I was also hoping for a little pick-me-up. Clara, do you have any chocolate-chip cookie dough back there? I just finished grading fifty essays on the economic impact of the Panama Canal. If I have to read the phrase 'a man-made marvel' one more time, I'll scream."

Gram chuckled, already heading for the case. "Sounds like you've earned it. I'll cast a quick spell on the dough to make it safe to eat raw."

Sadie grinned as Gram handed her a pint-sized tub and a spoon. "Three spoons, please. I'm a firm believer in sharing."

Sadie held up her spoon, her green eyes twinkling. I picked up my own spoon and tapped it lightly against hers. "Here's to a man, a plan, a canal—Panama."

Gram joined in, clinking her spoon against ours. "Cheers to that!"

Sadie passed the tub to me after taking the first bite, and soon the three of us were indulging in the guilty pleasure of raw cookie dough.

"How long will you be here in Enchanted Springs?" I asked between bites.

Sadie paused, the spoon in her hand mid-air. "As long as you need me," she said with a small smile. "I know this witch stuff feels overwhelming right now, but you're not alone. Saturn Return is rough, even without magic in the mix. Most people just get a divorce or a quarter-life crisis. We get... extra."

I stared at her. "Wait a minute. Does everyone in this town know about my Saturn Return?"

Sadie and Gram exchanged a look, clearly weighing how much to say.

"Not everyone," Gram admitted finally. "Just those of us in the paranormal community."

"Of course," I said, leaning back with a sigh. "Because nothing says small-town living like everyone knowing your business."

Gram smiled gently. "That's part of what makes Enchanted Springs special. It also means you have a built-in support system. You're not alone, Marley. You're part of something bigger now."

Sadie reached for another bite of cookie dough. "Like me! I'd be happy to show you a few spells whenever you're ready."

I set my spoon down, the weight of the day catching up to me. "Thanks. I appreciate that, really. But right now, I think what I need most is a nap."

Sadie laughed, pushing her glasses up the bridge of her nose. "Fair enough. Rest is important. Just know the offer stands."

I glanced at Gram, who was watching me with her quiet, knowing expression—the one she always wore when she was waiting for me to come to terms with something big.

It wasn't just exhaustion I was feeling. It was the unsettling sense that my life was shifting in ways I couldn't quite grasp yet.

"I'll hold you to that offer," I said finally, giving Sadie a small smile. "But later. After I've slept."

Chapter 11

Home Sweet Home

I LEFT THE BAKERY in a daze, my thoughts racing as I navigated the familiar streets of Enchanted Springs. The revelations of the day hung over me like a storm cloud. I'd come back to town to reconnect with my roots and capture the festival's charm through my lens—not to be thrust into a world of ghosts, witches, and weird ancestral legacies.

The quiet neighborhoods I drove through seemed untouched by time. Houses with wide porches sat nestled among old-growth trees, their gardens meticulously maintained, every flowerbed and picket fence a testament to small-town pride. String lights twinkled here and there, hinting at late-night conversations on porches. Yet, even as the familiar rhythm of the town tried to comfort me, the images on my camera haunted me.

No matter how much I wanted to believe Gram's words were some elaborate joke, deep down, I couldn't shake the feeling that she might be right.

Our family home sat just six blocks north of downtown, skirting the edges of the Magnolia University campus. Once a modest farmhouse surrounded by a thriving orange grove, it had grown over the years, expanding to make space for extended family.

The house loomed ahead, its wide wraparound porch glowing softly in the dim light. A trio of rocking chairs sat arranged like old friends, their seats cushioned with faded floral prints. Hanging baskets of ferns swayed gently in the breeze, their shadows dancing on the white clapboard siding.

I retrieved the spare key from its usual hiding spot under a garden gnome. Just for good measure, I patted the gnome's head. "You're not real now, too, are you?" Happily, he didn't reply.

When I unlocked the door, the scent of lemon polish and old wood greeted me, surrounding me with core memories of home.

A curved staircase rose gracefully from the entryway, its banister smooth and gleaming from decades of hands trailing along its length. Above it, a vintage crystal chandelier hung like a constellation, scattering tiny rainbows across the walls.

To my left, my stepfather's den waited, a dark and orderly space filled with leather-bound books and the faint scent of pipe tobacco. To the right, the front room was the complete opposite—a cozy haven of overstuffed sofas, a crackling fireplace, and shelves overflowing with books.

My footsteps echoed softly on the wooden floors as I walked down the hall, past the dining room and into the spacious kitchen, with Gram's room off to one side. From there, a simple back staircase led upstairs to my old room. The door creaked slightly as I pushed it open, revealing a space frozen in time.

Nothing had changed. Dappled sunlight streamed through lace curtains, casting golden patterns on the pastel walls. The antique brass bed stood proudly in the center of the room, its frame polished to a gentle glow. A cozy sitting area occupied one corner, two mismatched armchairs and a round ottoman arranged on a faded Persian rug. My bookshelf stood undisturbed, still lined with the books I'd loved in high school and college, their spines faded but intact.

Everything was the same—except for the Siamese kitten curled up at the foot of my bed.

She was impossibly tiny, her cream-and-chocolate fur sleek, her tail tucked around her like a question mark. For a moment, I thought she was asleep, until one green eye cracked open to study me.

"Well, hello there," I murmured, crouching down to meet her gaze. "Where did you come from?"

The kitten yawned, stretched languidly, then hopped off the bed with an elegance only cats could manage. She circled my feet, her purring loud and contented, as if we were lifelong friends.

"You're not shy, are you?" I said, reaching out my hand. She sniffed it briefly before pressing her head into my palm, demanding affection.

After a moment, she sauntered back onto the bed, curling into the same spot as if she belonged there. Her green eyes glinted with something almost knowing, and I could've sworn she was studying me.

"All right, little one," I said, kicking off my shoes. "But I think I need more than a cat nap."

I changed into an oversized sleep shirt and slid beneath the quilt, the kitten curling against my side with a warmth that soothed my frazzled nerves.

The day's revelations tumbled through my mind—Violet's dazzling, ghostly presence, Sadie's easy camaraderie, Gram's startling disclosure about our family's magical legacy. It was overwhelming, yet here, in the soft cocoon of my old room, it felt slightly less impossible.

As the sunlight faded, casting the room in a golden twilight, I felt the faintest tug of something greater. My lineage, my future—it was all waiting for me, just on the other side of sleep.

The kitten's soft purring tethered me to the moment, its rhythmic vibration pulling me toward dreams. And for the first time since I'd returned to Enchanted Springs, I felt like I was exactly where I needed to be.

Chapter 12

A New Dawn

Hours later, I slowly emerged from the cocoon of night, reluctant to leave the comforting haze of dreams. The kitten was gone, but I could still see a faint impression of the place she had been curled up on the blanket.

Morning sunlight filtered softly through the lace curtains, casting golden patterns on the walls and ceiling. For a blissful moment, the events of the previous day felt distant, like a story I'd read rather than lived.

Outside, the town was alive with sound. Songbirds were in full-throated chorus, filling the air with a medley of Carolina wrens' rapid trills, Northern cardinals' clear whistles of "cheer, cheer, cheer," and the occasional harsh screech of a blue jay, which shattered the harmony like an alarm clock you couldn't hit snooze on.

The symphony of birdsong was joined by another, equally enticing attraction: the unmistakable aroma of bacon, eggs, and coffee drifting up from the kitchen. My stomach growled in response, reminding me that, magical revelations or not, I still needed to eat.

I followed the scent downstairs, drawn like a moth to a flame—or, more accurately, like a groggy granddaughter to Gram's world-famous breakfast croissants.

As I stepped into the kitchen, I found Gram swaying gently to the tinny sound of an oldies tune crackling from the radio. She moved with practiced ease, flipping bacon with one hand while reaching for her coffee cup with the other.

"Morning, Gram," I mumbled, still thick with sleep.

She turned, her face lighting up with a warm smile. "Good morning, sunshine. You're just in time."

She handed me a plate with one of her signature breakfast sandwiches, the flaky crust golden and buttery, the cheese melted to perfection. My stomach growled again in anticipation as I slid into a chair at the kitchen table.

As I took my first bite, I mumbled around a mouthful of croissant, "There was a kitten in my room last night. I didn't know you'd adopted a cat."

Gram paused mid-sip, her eyes sparkling with something that looked suspiciously like amusement. "Was it a little Siamese kitten?"

I nodded, my curiosity growing.

"That's Twila," she said, her tone as casual as if she were discussing the weather. "She must have felt like meeting you, too."

I frowned, the name sparking even more questions. "Twila? So, she has a name. But whose cat is she?"

Gram set her coffee down and leaned against the counter, a smile tugging at her lips like she was enjoying a private joke. "She's usually Violet's companion, but Twila has her own way of doing things. She shows up where and when she pleases."

I mulled this over, my fork pausing mid-air. "How did she know I was here? That's quite the coincidence."

Gram chuckled softly, shaking her head. "Nothing in Enchanted Springs is ever just a coincidence, Marley."

Cryptic much? I filed that remark away with all the other strange things I'd learned in the last twenty-four hours.

We shifted to safer topics—like the day ahead—while I polished off my breakfast.

"I think I'll start with photos of Main Street," I said, chasing the last crumbs of croissant with my fork.

Gram nodded approvingly. "Just keep an open mind about what you see. This town has a way of surprising you."

As I stood to head upstairs and get dressed, Gram leaned in to kiss my cheek, her apron in hand. "Kate opened for me this morning so I could be here when you woke up, but you know there's no rest for the wicked!"

I laughed, her words following me as I got ready for the day.

Chapter 13

A Spirited Walk

OUT ON THE STREETS of Enchanted Springs, the rhythm of the town was as soothing as ever. Sunlight filtered through the canopy of ancient oaks lining Main Street, dappling the sidewalks in patches of light and shadow.

But I couldn't help noticing that the world didn't look quite the same anymore. I was surrounded by ghosts.

Now that Gram had told me the truth, it was impossible not to see them—those faintly glowing figures moving among the living. At first glance, they blended in seamlessly: a woman in a wide-brimmed hat adjusting her gloves near a storefront, a man in a pinstripe suit tipping his hat to a passerby. But their ethereal glow gave them away, as if they were illuminated by some soft, heavenly aura.

I wondered if I'd always seen them and just assumed they were ordinary people. This morning, I could tell the difference.

The ghosts seemed content to go about their business, paying little attention to me. Most acted as though they were still alive, moving through the world with the same purpose and routines they must have had when they walked it in flesh.

Was this my life now? Surrounded by spirits everywhere I looked? It was distracting, to say the least.

As I strolled toward downtown, I tried to push the questions aside and focus on the familiar sights of Main Street. I let the steady rhythm of my hometown soothe me, choosing the comfort of the present over the mysteries of the past.

I found myself walking past Sheridan Real Estate and decided to stop in. In high school, Ivy Sheridan had been one of my best friends. Now she was one of Enchanted Springs's top real-estate agents, and by the look of her building, business was booming.

Her office occupied a landmark corner on Main Street and Addison Avenue, housed in what had once been the town's grandest bank. The front entrance was framed by Roman columns, lending it an air of timeless authority that practically screamed trustworthy.

Inside, the space was a masterclass in modern luxury wrapped in historic charm. Marble floors gleamed like a mirror under the soft glow of chandeliers. A row of preserved teller windows stood as decorative nods to the building's past, while the old walk-in vault had been transformed into an office coffee bar. Its massive iron door stood open, revealing shelves lined with gleaming mugs, jars of tea, and a state-of-the-art espresso machine that hummed faintly in the background.

Above it all, the ceiling featured a sprawling fresco of Greek gods and goddesses lounging on clouds, their immortal revelry adding an unexpected playfulness to the room's elegance.

I stepped inside, following the ghost of a businessman dressed in a three-piece suit, a leather briefcase in hand. He moved with purpose, striding confidently through the glass doors without bothering to open them. I paused, watching as he passed through a solid wall and disappeared. A shiver crept down my spine, but I forced myself to shake it off. Just a ghost, I reminded myself. Nothing to be afraid of.

"Marley Montgomery!"

Ivy's voice drew my attention, and before I could respond, she was already in the reception area, pulling me into a tight hug.

"I didn't know you were back in town!" she exclaimed, stepping back to study me. Concern flickered across her face. "Wait. Is Clara okay? She's not sick, is she?"

I smiled, touched by her worry. "No, she's fine. Happy and healthy. I'm the one going through some changes."

Her brow furrowed slightly, and she motioned for me to follow her to a seating area near the back. "Oh dear. All good, I hope?"

I sank into a plush leather sofa while Ivy settled into a matching armchair. As always, I was struck by her beauty. Her long, dark hair cascaded in glossy waves over her shoulders, framing high cheekbones and full lips. Her blue eyes, bright and vibrant, were accented by mauve shadow and impossibly thick lashes.

Her assistant, Natalie, appeared with two steaming cups of coffee, setting them on the table between us. Ivy glanced up with a grateful smile. "Thanks, Natalie."

I looked around, taking in the space. When Ivy first started her career, she worked out of a tiny office in a strip mall, wedged between a nail salon and a pizza parlor.

"This is definitely an upgrade from your last place," I said with a grin.

She shrugged modestly, but her eyes sparkled with pride. "What can I say? I'm a very good real-estate agent."

I wasn't surprised. Back in high school, Ivy had been one of the popular girls, but not for the usual reasons. She wasn't admired just because she was beautiful or because she was a cheerleader and homecoming queen. Ivy had been popular because she was kind. She made everyone feel like they belonged—even the kids no one else wanted to talk to. Ivy didn't have a clique; she had her own orbit, and everyone was welcome in it.

"So, what brings you back to Enchanted Springs?" she asked, her tone light but curious. "Was it Trent?"

I rolled my eyes. "No. Trent is old news. Honestly, breaking up with him was the best thing that could've happened. It gave me the push I needed to go freelance."

Her grin widened, and she held up her hand for a high five. "Way to go, fellow business owner!"

I laughed, slapping her hand. "Thanks. It's been great so far—challenging, but worth it."

Her expression softened, and she leaned forward slightly, her gaze intent. "Marley, it's so good to see you back. Enchanted Springs has missed you."

I paused, unsure how to respond. There was something in her tone, something that made me feel like she could see more than I was saying.

"So, how long are you planning to stay?" she asked, her question casual but probing.

I stirred my coffee, the motion giving me a moment to think. "I don't know, honestly," I admitted, the truth spilling out before I could stop it. "My job gives me some flexibility, so I might stick around for a bit. There's a lot for me to figure out here."

Her eyes lingered on me for a moment before she smiled, a knowing, supportive smile that reminded me why she'd been such a good friend. "Well, if you need anything—anything at all—you know where to find me."

Chapter 14

Opal Hush

AFTER MY IMPROMPTU COFFEE with Ivy, I kept walking, camera in hand. As I strolled south along the thorough-fare, I found more to photograph than I would have thought possible. I guess I'd been away just long enough to see my hometown with fresh eyes.

The old brick buildings that lined both sides of the street stood like sentinels of another era, their weathered facades and colorful awnings steeped in history. Picture windows showcased everything from books to handcrafted jewelry, each display an invitation to pause and peer into a world preserved in time.

I snapped photos as I walked, capturing the light as it played off antique lampposts, the soft curves of wrought-iron balconies, and the glow of the cobblestone street beneath the late-afternoon sun.

The charm of Main Street was undeniable. The brightly painted shop signs, the carefully tended flower boxes, the way the community seemed to hum with quiet pride—it all felt like home, yet new and alive in a way I hadn't noticed before.

Still, despite the soothing rhythm of my surroundings, I couldn't shake the strange, jittery energy that had settled over me since I'd arrived.

By the time I reached the southern edge of the business district, I found myself drawn to the Springs Hotel once again.

I stopped in front of the building, tilting my head to study it. Its Spanish Revival façade glowed warmly in the sunlight, its arched windows glinting like secrets waiting to be uncovered. I was a little wary of repeating yesterday's experience, but the promise of a cool drink was impossible to resist.

I headed toward the old check-in desk that was now a sleek bar. I slid onto stool at the far end, setting my camera on the counter as the bartender approached.

"What can I get you?" he asked, his tone polite and unhurried.

I hesitated for a moment. I wasn't on vacation, exactly, but I wasn't tied to the clock, either. A little day drinking couldn't hurt.

The bar's signature cocktail called out to me. "I'll have an Opal Hush," I said

He nodded, turning to begin crafting the drink. I watched as he poured a splash of deep red claret wine into a glass, the liquid swirling like a ruby. Next came an effervescent spritz of sparkling lemonade, the bubbles fizzing brightly as they met the wine.

The result was a perfectly layered drink, its rich crimson base lightening into a sunny gold at the top.

I was about to compliment the drink when the air around me shifted.

Oh no. Not again.

The hum of conversation faded into a muffled echo. The light in the room dimmed, shifting into a sepia-toned haze that drained the color from everything around me. My breath hitched as the modern décor melted away, replaced by the Springs Hotel lobby as it looked decades ago.

Was this my life now? Was I going to be shifting through time all the time? The thought sent a flicker of panic through me, but I didn't have long to dwell on it.

The faint scent of tobacco and old wood mingled with the strains of swing music drifting from a distant radio. Women in fitted dresses and men in polished suits moved through the space with purpose, their conversations blending into a soft murmur beneath the music.

Behind the check-in desk stood a short, balding clerk, his thick-framed glasses glinting under the grand chandelier.

The redheaded woman swept into view, a string of pearls gleaming against her neck and a ruby brooch catching the light with every step. Instinct took over again, and I raised my camera.

The click of the shutter felt too loud in the subdued space, but I didn't care. I snapped the photo just as she turned her head, her eyes locking onto mine. She froze, her lips parting as if to speak—but before she could, the vision shattered like glass.

I was back in the wine bar.

The hum of conversation rushed in, drowning out the swing music, and the room's modern glow replaced the sepia tones. My heart raced as I glanced at the camera screen. There she was, frozen mid-step, her every detail captured in stunning clarity.

"Here you go," the bartender said, sliding my drink across the counter. "One Opal Hush."

I nodded absently, lifting the glass to my lips. The refreshing tang of lemonade mingled with the richness of claret, but I could barely register the flavors.

My gaze drifted across the room—and my stomach flipped.

The redheaded woman was still there, now by the window, her silhouette framed by the setting sun. She watched me, her expression unreadable, and for a moment, the world seemed to tilt.

"Marley, are you all right?"

A familiar voice steadied me, and I turned to see Sadie Arragon standing at my side. Her crisp white shirt and tailored trousers were effortlessly stylish, but it was her piercing green eyes that held my attention. She reached out, steadying me with a hand on my arm.

"You look like you've seen a ghost," she said lightly, her tone tinged with concern.

I blinked, glancing back toward the window. The redheaded woman was gone.

"I think I did," I whispered.

Chapter 15

Photos of the Past

"COME ON," SADIE SAID gently, guiding me away from the bar and toward a secluded table tucked in the back. "Let's sit down and have a bite to eat. You look like you could use it."

I followed her to a cozy corner where the noise of the wine bar softened to a low hum. The walls around us were adorned with black-and-white photographs of the Springs Hotel in its heyday. Elegant couples posed on the grand staircase, and horse-drawn buggies lined Main Street in others. Vibrant paintings of Enchanted Springs were scattered among the photos, their lively brushstrokes a stark contrast to the vintage images.

The dining area was as effortlessly chic as the rest of the wine bar. Polished dark wood tables were set with linen napkins and tiny vases of fresh flowers, while pendant lights cast golden pools of warmth across the room. The soft notes of jazz completed the bubble of calm.

Still clutching my camera, I flipped through the images until Colette's striking profile appeared on the screen. "Okay," I said, holding it out to Sadie. "You've got to see this. Tell me this isn't bizarre."

Sadie leaned in, her green eyes narrowing as she studied the photo. "It's incredible. You're literally capturing moments in time—but they're obviously from the past. I've never seen anything like it."

She handed the camera back. "You know," she murmured, tracing the screen with her fingertip, "if I could time travel, my historical research would be so much easier." She sighed wistfully, propping her chin on her hand. "Instead, I'm just a humble spellcaster, forever stuck in the here and now."

I brushed my fingers across the top of the camera. "Is this something that happens to witches? Because if it is, I need a heads-up for the next time a ghost wants a photo op."

Sadie grinned. "It's rare, but not unheard of. Enchanted Springs isn't your average town, and you're not your average witch."

"Still not used to hearing that word," I said, sitting back with a huff. "But I guess that explains why my camera's suddenly a magical time machine. Great. Love that for me."

Sadie laughed lightly. "Your camera's not magic, Marley. You are. The camera's just riding your coattails."

Before I could argue, a familiar voice interrupted.

"Marley Montgomery?"

I looked up to see Scarlett Linden approaching, her sharp features and sleek style impossible to miss. Her jet-black hair was parted down the middle and tied into a smooth ponytail at the nape of her neck, emphasizing her sculpted cheekbones and flawless makeup. She looked like she'd stepped straight out of a magazine ad—polished, confident, and completely unflappable.

"Scarlett," I said, sitting up straighter. "It's been ages."

"It has," she said warmly, stopping at our table. "I didn't know you were back in town! Your parents must be thrilled."

"They're on sabbatical," I explained. "Off chasing the legend of some mythical priestess in Central America."

Scarlett chuckled. "That sounds exactly like Ava and Cliff." Her gaze dropped to the camera in my lap. "Still taking pictures, I see."

I didn't have a chance to respond before her eyes snagged on the image of Colette displayed on the screen. She tilted her head, her expression shifting from curious to genuinely surprised.

"That's Colette Rios," she said. "You must've been to the History Center already."

As she spoke, I remembered hearing about Scarlett's connection to this place. A few years ago, she'd bought the Springs Hotel and poured herself into transforming it. The lounge had been expanded, the lobby reimagined as this stunning wine bar. Scarlett had given the historic building a second life, and it showed in every detail.

I didn't want to reveal my secret, so I answered with a question of my own. "What do you know about her?"

Scarlett smiled, more than happy to share. "She owned this hotel back in the '40s. She was a real trailblazer—took over from her father and turned the place into a luxury destination when women in business were practically unheard of."

"She sounds impressive," I said, glancing at the photo again.

"She was," Scarlett agreed, but her tone dipped into something quieter. "And then, in 1945, she vanished. No warning, no trace. Just gone."

A chill prickled my skin. "Vanished?"

Scarlett nodded, leaning against the edge of the table. "Some said she ran off with a lover, others thought it was foul play. The truth is, no one knows what happened to her. The whole thing's been a mystery for decades."

The words hung in the air, but Scarlett shook them off with a bright smile. "Anyway, enough about that. Are you two here for lunch? Our sandwiches are excellent—just saying."

Sadie perked up immediately. "Oh, you mean the veggie wraps? They're my favorite. You haven't lived until you've had one."

Scarlett laughed. "They're good, but the grilled cheese? That's what people come back for. Three cheeses, locally made sourdough, and a raspberry and red onion chutney." She winked. "It's practically famous."

"I'm in," I said, already imagining the crispy, gooey perfection.

"Make it two," Sadie added. "But hold the chutney on mine."

Scarlett smiled warmly. "Coming right up."

As she walked away, Sadie looked back at me. "A mythical priestess, huh?"

"Yeah," I said, leaning back into the cushions. "Mom's convinced they've found some matriarchal society where rituals and magic were a way of life. She calls it groundbreaking. Cliff calls it complicated."

Sadie smiled faintly, her eyes glinting. "Sounds like magic, power, and complicated women are a theme in your life."

I snorted. "Apparently so."

Sadie's laugh was soft, but it made the air between us lighter. "Good thing you're here, then. Sounds like Enchanted Springs might have a few answers waiting for you."

Chapter 16

History's Mysteries

S ADIE LEANED BACK IN her chair, her gaze sweeping the room with an appreciative nod. "I have to say, this old hotel has a lot of charm. Of course, it's not nearly as old as some inns back home in Salem."

I raised an eyebrow, intrigued. "Salem, Massachusetts? That's quite the change from Enchanted Springs. What brought you here?"

She grinned, a flicker of mischief lighting up her green eyes. "Well, aside from filling in for your mother, which is a step up in my teaching career, I'm also hear to learn more about Enchanted Springs. I needed a break from Salem's magical community. I love it ther, but it definitely has a few quirks. Let's just say things can get complicated."

"Complicated how?" I asked, leaning forward.

Sadie chuckled softly, tucking a strand of platinum-blonde hair behind her ear. "In Salem, witches are practically a tourist attraction. The legends, the kitschy ghost tours, the whole vibe—living there feels like being in a fishbowl. Don't get me wrong, it's home, and I love it, but sometimes you need a break from the broomstick jokes."

I laughed, picturing Sadie surrounded by tourists wearing witch hats and snapping selfies. "So you came here for a change of pace?"

"More than that," she said, her voice turning thoughtful. "I wanted to see how other magical communities live. How they balance magic with the mundane. Your mom's leave from Magnolia University was perfect timing. Filling in for her gave me a chance to dig into the history and energy of this town."

Her gaze drifted toward the window as though she could see the roots of the town stretching beneath us. "Salem taught me the foundations of magic, but Enchanted Springs is different. There's a harmony here, a natural rhythm. It's like the magic and the land are part of the same breath."

I studied her, unsure whether to feel flattered or freaked out. "So you're a witch studying other witches? That's an interesting angle."

She laughed, the sound light and genuine. "You could say that. Each magical community has its own personality. Its own way of weaving magic into everyday life. But Enchanted Springs is special. Here, magic isn't just a part of life—it's part of the town's DNA."

Scarlett returned with our lunch, setting down plates that smelled like heaven. Sadie took a bite of her grilled cheese and sighed in contentment. I tried mine, too. The balance of gooey cheese and tangy chutney made me close my eyes in bliss. "Okay, this might be the best grilled cheese I've ever had. Scarlett's a genius."

"Agreed," Sadie said, dabbing her napkin at the corner of her mouth. "But back to what I was saying—this town's history and magic are so intertwined, you can't separate one from the other. It's like trying to pull apart the roots of those oaks outside without bringing up half the town with them."

I nodded, chewing thoughtfully as her words sank in. The idea of magic being woven into the foundation of Enchanted Springs was unsettling—but it also made a strange kind of sense.

A brief lull gave me a chance to glance at my camera. Sadie noticed, her green eyes sharpening with curiosity. "Let me see that photo again."

I hesitated but turned the screen toward her. The red-headed woman stared back at us, her eyes filled with something urgent and unknowable.

Sadie studied the image for a long moment, her expression unreadable. "She's more than a ghost," she said finally. "She's a story. And something tells me you're meant to finish it."

I handed my camera to Sadie, watching as she studied the image on the viewscreen with a focus that bordered on reverence.

Sadie's green eyes flicked up to meet mine. "We both know you didn't take this at the History Center. Where were you when you saw her?"

I hesitated, then shook my head, pushing the photo closer to her as though the answer might reveal itself in the pixels. "I was here, in the hotel."

As I recounted the moment, the memory pulled me back in like a tide. "It wasn't just seeing her," I said, my voice quieter. "It felt like I stepped out of time. Everything shifted. The air smelled different—like cedar and old books—and the sounds changed. I could hear swing music playing, the rustle of papers at the check-in desk, even the faint clink of glasses. It wasn't just a glimpse of the past. I felt like I was there."

Sadie leaned forward, her expression sharpening with intrigue. "That's not just ordinary magic, Marley. That's extraordinary."

"Extraordinary?" I echoed, half-laughing. "It's extraordinary that I don't have whiplash. These time shifts are random, and I have zero control over them."

Sadie grinned, her enthusiasm unfazed. "Agreed," she repeated firmly. "It is extraordinary. Capturing spirit images with this level of clarity? That's rare, even among witches. And the time shifts? That's something else entirely. It's like you're tethered to the past and present at the same time."

"Sounds more like I'm tangled in it," I muttered, sinking back into my seat. "I can't even tell when it's going to happen, let alone why."

Her gaze softened, and she reached across the table to lay a steadying hand over mine. "It's a gift, Marley. A rare and powerful one. Gifts like this come with a responsibility—but they also come with answers. You just need the right tools and guidance to uncover them."

I let her words settle, though they felt heavy, like I was trying to hold onto a balloon in a hurricane. "So where do I even start? How do I figure out what happened to Colette?"

Sadie's eyes gleamed, her tone brightening with excitement. "That's where I come in. I've got full access to Magnolia University's archives—everything from old newspaper clippings to personal journals. If Colette left a trace, I'll find it."

Her confidence was infectious, and I felt a flicker of hope. "Won't people wonder what you're up to?"

She plucked an olive from the charcuterie board with a flourish. "Please. No one questions a professor in a library. And if they do? I'll say I'm researching for the Founders Festival. History buffs eat that up."

I laughed despite myself. "Good cover."

She tilted her head, her expression thoughtful. "But before I start digging, I need to know more about what you're experiencing. These shifts—are there patterns? Anything you feel before they happen?"

I considered her question, my brow furrowing. "Not really. They're so random. One minute, I'm in the present, and the next,

I'm surrounded by ghosts in vintage clothes. Sometimes there's a trigger, like my camera, but not always. It's disorienting."

Sadie nodded, her fingers tapping absently against her glass. "That makes sense. Your magic's new, so it's raw—unfocused. You haven't learned to channel it yet."

Her words landed with a mixture of relief and apprehension. "So it's possible to control this?"

"Absolutely," she said, her confidence unwavering. "It'll take time and practice, but you'll get there. In the meantime, you've got me to help figure out the history side of things."

Scarlett returned, clearing our plates with a friendly smile. As she walked away, Sadie glanced at her watch, the gesture snapping me back to the present.

"Marley," she said, her voice steady and encouraging, "what you're dealing with—it's just the beginning. But understanding your gift, learning to harness it, takes time and guidance. The more we uncover about Colette, the more you'll understand what you're capable of."

Chapter 17

The Edge of Night

B ACK HOME, THE EVENING had settled into a comfortable
silence, broken only by the occasional creak of the old house
and the faint rustle of wind through the magnolia trees. The
familiar sounds wrapped around me like a favorite sweater as I
wandered into the family room.

Gram sat in her favorite chair, a worn but elegant armchair by the
bay window. A book lay forgotten in her lap, its pages fluttering
slightly in the breeze from the oscillating fan. She gazed out at the
moonlit garden, where the soft glow of fireflies danced like tiny
stars caught on earth.

I pulled up a chair beside her, the cushions sinking under me
as I opened my camera. "Grandma, look at this," I said, tilting
the screen so she could see. The photo of Colette Rios glowed
brightly, her poised figure frozen mid-step. "I took this today at
Opal Hush. Scarlett Linden recognized her—she said her name's
Colette Rios. She disappeared at the end of World War Two."

Gram leaned closer, her keen eyes narrowing as she studied the image. "Oh, Marley," she murmured, her voice carrying a mix of wonder and sadness. "Colette's story is one of Enchanted Springs' greatest unsolved mysteries. It happened before my time, but people still whisper about her."

I watched her expression shift, the flicker of memory and thought crossing her face. "Sadie's offered to research her disappearance in the university archives. She thinks we might find something new."

Gram nodded, her lips curving into a small, approving smile. "That's good. Sadie's thorough—she's the kind of person who leaves no stone unturned. But you know, it might also help to speak with Jack Edgewood."

"Who's that?"

She turned her gaze to me, a spark of amusement in her eyes. "Jack's a detective with the Enchanted Springs police department. He knows this town's history as well as anyone. If there's anything to be known about Colette, he might have some insight."

I filed the name away, making a mental note to reach out. "I'll think about it," I said, though the idea of interrogating a local detective about a ghostly photo made me feel a little ridiculous.

A soft meow pulled my attention toward the doorway. Twila, the spectral Siamese kitten, sat primly in the shadows, her blue eyes glowing faintly in the dim light.

"Hey, Twila," I whispered, not wanting to startle her.

She meowed again, a delicate, inviting sound, and padded toward the staircase. Her tail flicked once, a clear signal.

Gram chuckled, watching the interaction with her usual calm amusement. "I think she's telling you it's time for bed."

I yawned, the events of the day catching up with me all at once. "She's not wrong. It's been a long day."

As Gram picked up her book and turned back to the garden view, I stood and followed Twila upstairs. Each step creaked underfoot, the old house settling into its nightly rhythm. Twila glanced back at me every few steps, her tiny form leading the way like a spectral tour guide.

At the top of the stairs, she stopped outside my bedroom door, sitting perfectly still as if waiting for me to open it. When I did, she padded inside and leapt onto the bed with effortless grace.

"Are you tucking me in now?" I teased, watching her curl into a neat ball at the foot of the bed. Her blue eyes blinked at me once, slowly, before drifting closed.

Shaking my head at the absurdity—and magic—of it all, I changed into my favorite nightshirt and climbed under the quilt. The room was bathed in soft moonlight, its silver glow lending a dreamlike quality to the familiar space.

Twila's steady purring filled the quiet, a soothing counterpoint to my swirling thoughts. As the events of the day replayed in my mind—Colette's photo, Sadie's enthusiasm, Gram's quiet certainty—I felt the weight of it settle. It was heavy, yes, but not unbearable.

The last thing I saw before sleep claimed me was Twila, her tiny form bathed in moonlight, a quiet reminder that even in the strangest moments, there was magic.

Chapter 18

The Enchanted Antique Shop

T HE MORNING SUN POURED through my bedroom window, golden and warm, washing away the last remnants of my dreams. Twila was gone, though a faint warmth lingered at the foot of my bed where she'd slept.

My dreams had been strange—hidden doors, whispered secrets—but they dissolved like mist as I stretched and swung my legs over the side of the bed.

Today was the start of something new. Eleanor had invited me to the Enchanted Antique Shop for what she called the beginning of my "formal magical education." Gram had promised to join us later, after the bakery's morning rush.

By the time I arrived, the shop's familiar facade greeted me with its timeless charm. The hand-painted sign swung lazily in the breeze, the gold lettering catching the sunlight. But the door was locked.

I frowned, leaning closer to peer through the glass. Inside, shadows pooled in the corners, the usual golden glow replaced by an eerie dimness. The ornate mirror that usually reflected the morning light was dull and gray, as if it had forgotten how to shine.

"Eleanor?" I called, knocking gently. The sound was flat, swallowed by the strange stillness.

Just as I turned to head toward the bakery for help, there was a soft click. I spun back to see the door creak open, Eleanor standing there with a confused look in her eyes.

"Oh, hello, Marley!" she said brightly, though her tone carried a faint edge of tension. She flipped the light switch, bathing the shop in its usual warm glow. Before I could say a single word, she reached out and took both my hands.

"Come in, dear," she said, her grip surprisingly firm as she pulled me inside. "I'm sorry I wasn't here to greet you earlier. Violet let me know that you were at the door."

Violet. The mention of the ghost sent a shiver through me. To my mind, she was the one who started all this—but Eleanor bustled ahead, leaving me to follow in her wake.

She seemed off, somehow. Her movements were stiff, her smile strained. Her eyes darted around the room as though she were looking for something—or someone.

"Are you feeling alright, Eleanor?" I asked carefully.

She waved off the question with a laugh that felt too bright. "Oh, I'm fine, dear. Just fine. And now that you're here, I feel even better."

Looping her arm through mine, she led me deeper into the shop. The front room unfolded like a Victorian parlor, filled with delicate furniture and treasures from another era.

"It's been a while since you've visited," she said, her tone cheery. "Let me show you some of our more intriguing items."

We stopped at a glass dome that housed a wax doll. Its curls were delicate, its stiff features frozen in an eerie half-smile.

"This beauty dates back to 1810," Eleanor said, tapping the glass. "Original dress, pantaloons, and shoes. Perfectly preserved." Her eyes gleamed with a strange pride. "You'd think she could blink, wouldn't you?"

I laughed nervously, but there was something unsettling about the doll's lifeless gaze.

Eleanor moved to a shelf and picked up a ball-and-cup toy. With practiced ease, she flicked the ball into the air and caught it on the cup's edge. "Primitive, but delightful," she said. "Rumor has it this toy belonged to Winston Churchill himself. And I have it on good authority he still stops by occasionally to check on it."

She handed it to me, and as my fingers closed around the smooth mahogany, a faint vibration hummed against my palm. I jerked slightly, startled.

"Did you feel that?" I asked, holding the toy out like it might jump out of my had.

She shrugged. "Some objects carry a little bit of their owner's essence. It's nothing to be afraid of."

We continued through the shop, her stories as fascinating as the treasures she displayed. A porcelain tea set revealed a hidden geisha when held to the light. An oil painting of George Cheddar, a spiritualist from the 1880s, seemed to watch me as we walked past.

Finally, we stopped at a mahogany table set for tea, every detail perfectly curated down to the embroidered napkins. The light shifted slightly, catching the silver teapot, and for a moment, I could've sworn I saw steam rising from its spout.

Eleanor placed a hand on my shoulder, her gaze piercing. "Magic is everywhere in this shop, Marley. Some of it is dormant, waiting to be awakened. Some of it hums beneath the surface, like a heartbeat."

Eleanor gestured to a carved wooden chair across from her and settled gracefully into her own, her posture so upright and poised it was as if she'd stepped out of a Victorian portrait. "Sit, Marley," she said, her tone warm but firm. "We have so much to discuss. Would you like some tea, dear?"

I nodded, feeling oddly formal in the presence of her effortless elegance.

With a delicate wave of her hand, Eleanor motioned toward the flowered teapot in the center of the table. To my astonishment, the price tags tied to it untied themselves and floated gently to the side like leaves caught on a soft breeze.

I gasped in astonishment as the teapot levitated. It tipped with precision, pouring steaming chamomile tea into my cup. The sweet, herbal aroma wafted up, soothing and inviting. The pot floated gracefully to Eleanor's cup next, where it poured a distinctly darker brew. The citrusy scent of Earl Grey curled through the air.

I stared at the teapot, then at Eleanor, my expression apparently betraying my astonishment.

"Did you not want chamomile, dear?" she asked, raising an elegant brow in concern.

"No, it's my favorite," I admitted quickly. "But how did you do that?"

She shrugged, a playful twinkle in her eye, and gestured with her hand. "It's all in the wrist."

Before I could respond, the chair to my left slid out from the table with a soft, deliberate scrape against the floor. My heart leapt as the air shimmered, faint motes of golden light gathering until they coalesced into a shape. The mysterious woman from the fountain—and the beach—materialized with a dramatic flourish.

Her 1920s fringed dress swayed as she settled into the chair, every bead and sequin catching the light in a way that made her seem both ethereal and dazzlingly real. Beaded accessories jingled softly as she moved, and her red lipstick was as bold as her easy confidence.

Eleanor's face lit with a mixture of amusement and anticipation. "Marley, dear," she said, her voice brimming with affection, "there's someone I believe you've already met, albeit not formally. Allow me to introduce Miss Violet Serrano."

"Charmed, I'm sure," Violet said, her voice carrying the lilting cadence of a Jazz Age starlet. Her ruby lips curved into a knowing smile. "Though it seems we keep bumping into each other at the most interesting moments."

I nearly dropped my teacup, my reflexes just sharp enough to save it from disaster. "It's nice to meet you properly, Violet. I guess third time's the charm?"

Violet laughed, the sound like a cascade of wind chimes caught in a summer breeze. "Indeed! Though, I must say, our previous encounters were quite the showstoppers. A beach photoshoot and a spectral cameo at the fountain? We make a great team, Toots!"

Eleanor chuckled, clearly entertained by the exchange. "Violet is quite the character," she said, her tone fond. "She's been part of Enchanted Springs' story for a long time. And she has a knack for showing up when you least expect her."

"I prefer to think of it as impeccable timing," Violet said with a playful wink. Her translucent form shimmered faintly as she glanced toward the door. "And speaking of timing, here comes your grandmother."

I turned toward the door just as it swung open, the tinkling bell above announcing Gram's arrival. She looked unbothered by the late-morning heat, her usual grace intact as she stepped into the shop.

She paused, surveying the scene before her with a pleased smile. "Ah, the gang's all here. But how is it you're having tea without a bite of something sweet to go with it?"

She set a pink bakery box on the table and opened the lid to reveal an assortment of bite-size cookies, cupcakes, and delicate little tarts.

"Clara, darling!" Violet sang, rising from her chair with an exuberant twirl. "It's been too long. Still keeping these mortals in line?"

"Someone has to," Gram replied smoothly. She took a seat and waited patiently while the magic teapot hovered in midair and poured her a cup of mint tea, steaming and aromatic. "Now, let's not forget the reason we're all here. Marley, you might be a new witch, but it's not a moment too soon to start your training."

Violet laughed, a musical sound that seemed to ripple through the air. "Training. Pffft. Let's just throw her into the deep end and see if she floats."

Eleanor shook her head. "We've asked you not to mix metaphors, Violet, and any talk of throwing witches into water is in poor taste in present company."

Violet shrugged. "Gotcha."

Clara leaned forward. "Magic's not just about fancy teapots and disappearing ghosts. It's about connection—past, present, and future." She leaned forward conspiratorially, her translucent form shimmering faintly. "And in case you hadn't noticed, you're right at the center of it all."

I blinked, glancing around for confirmation. "Is this true? Why does everyone keep saying I'm the center of something?"

Gram nodded. "Because it's true. The Montgomery family has always been deeply connected to Enchanted Springs. It's why we've stayed here for generations. And you, Marley, are a pivotal part of that legacy. Your magic isn't just a gift—it's a key to unlocking the town's secrets."

"Secrets like Colette's disappearance?"

"Exactly," Gram said, her eyes glinting as she briefed Eleanor and Violet on the story. "The threads of her life are tangled up with the magic of this town. Finding the truth about what happened to her could unravel much more than you realize."

Violet perched on the edge of her chair, her enthusiasm palpable. "And lucky for you, Toots, you've got me! Nobody knows this town's history like I do. After all, I lived it."

I shook my head. "This is a lot to take in."

Violet broke the silence with a theatrical clap of her hands. "Exactly! You've got magic, a mystery to solve, and me as your guide. What more could a girl ask for?"

I couldn't help but laugh, the sound surprising even me. "A manual might be nice," I said wryly.

Chapter 19

Time for Tea

"I HAVE SO MANY questions. How does all this work? What am I supposed to do?"

Eleanor's eyes twinkled. "For now, let's start with the basics. You clearly have the ability to see and interact with the past. It's a rare gift—one that can reveal secrets and stories long forgotten. It's a gift your daughter shares, too."

Grandma Clara gently set her teacup down on the matching saucer and cleared her throat. "No, Eleanor. She doesn't have a child yet. That's still in the future."

Eleanor chuckled wryly. "Of course! Oh, sometimes my time-traveling mind plays tricks on me."

Gram passed me the plate of cookies, but I couldn't help noticing a flicker of something behind Eleanor's amused expression—a moment of disconnect, like a thread slipping loose from the fabric of reality.

The two shared a look of mutual understanding, then turned to me with synchronized nods.

"There's no need to rush your training," Gram said, helping herself to a bite-sized brownie. "For now, we'll ease you into it. After all, you'll have the rest of your life to master your gifts."

"With plenty of snacks along the way," Eleanor added, reaching for a lemon tart.

Gram gestured around the shop with a thoughtful expression. "You know, time has a way of waiting for us, especially in places like this." Her gaze lingered on the timeless antiques around us. "Here, the past and present mingle like old friends, unchanged by the years that pass outside these walls."

I glanced around, suddenly aware of just how true that was. The Enchanted Antique Shop had always been a mainstay on Main Street, its presence unwavering while other small businesses came and went. As a child, I'd visited a few times with Gram, but I'd never really thought about it. Now that I did, I realized that nothing inside had ever changed.

"How long has this shop been here?"

"Since Enchanted Springs was founded," Gram said. "It was originally the Mercantile, a general store that carried everything new homesteaders couldn't build or make for themselves—coffee, flour, bolts of fabric, kitchenware. It was one of the few brick buildings in town, which is why it survived the Great Fire that destroyed most of Main Street back in 1888."

Eleanor nodded solemnly. "Oh, that was a terrible fire."

"I remember," Gram added, shaking her head. "The sparks flying, the sound... People don't realize how loud a fire can be."

I blinked. "Eleanor, how could you remember a fire in 1888?" I did some quick math. "And if you really are a hundred and twenty years old, are you sure you could even remember it?"

Eleanor grunted indignantly. "We remember it because we were there, of course."

I opened my mouth, then closed it again. I'd seen enough in Enchanted Springs to not discount anything outright.

"Are you talking about photos?" I asked skeptically.

Eleanor waved a dismissive hand. "Photos? Mere shadows of light. We're talking about seeing living history, Marley."

The two of them exchanged a knowing glance. Eleanor smiled slyly. "Are you thinking what I'm thinking?"

Gram smacked her hand against the table. "Spectacular idea, my dear! Though that fire was so tragic. Let's show her something more pleasant, like the Founders Festival!"

I frowned. "But the festival doesn't start until this weekend."

"Oh, we're not talking about this year's festival," Eleanor said with a mischievous grin. "I think we should visit one of the first festivals, back when most of the old pioneers were still on this side of the veil."

"Exactly! Some of those parades were better than any modern-day contrivances."

I blinked, surprised but undeniably intrigued. The idea of stepping directly into history sent a thrill down my spine.

Violet floated slightly above her chair, her expression thoughtful. "I think I'll hang back this time. I've seen plenty of the past. I'm all about the present now."

Her decision was met with nods of agreement.

"All right then, it's settled," Gram said, her eyes twinkling with anticipation. "Prepare yourself, Marley. You're about to experience the Founders Festival in a way few ever have."

Then Gram turned momentarily serious. "What you're about to experience is open to only a chosen few. What you will see can only be shared among fellow travelers."

Eleanor bobbed her head good-naturedly. "Actually, we're not even sure if you'll be able to travel with us!" She laughed. "Well, we're pretty sure, but now is as good a time as any to find out."

I swallowed hard, gripping my teacup a little tighter. "No pressure, then."

Violet raised her glass in a mock toast. "To history, magic, and whatever mischief you two are about to get us into."

Gram clinked her cup against Violet's with a wink. "To the past—and the granddaughter who's about to walk straight into it."

Chapter 20

The Rules of Time Travel

G RAM CLEARED HER THROAT, her expression uncharac-
teristically serious. "Marley, there are rules to this—fun-
damentals we must adhere to when we traverse through time."

Eleanor nodded, leaning forward, her gaze locking with mine.
"First and foremost, you must never do anything that could
alter the timeline. Even the smallest action can ripple out in
ways we can't predict. It's not just about avoiding major historical events; even minor interactions can have unintended
consequences."

"Exactly," Gram continued, her tone steady and deliberate.
"And you must never reveal the future to anyone in the past.
No matter how much you might want to change something
or warn someone, you must keep what you know to yourself.
The future is a book that should remain closed."

Eleanor took a deliberate sip of her tea, her eyes sharp and focused. "And remember, Marley, you're an observer. The past isn't

a place to live in—it's a place to learn from. Watch, study, and return with that knowledge intact. Nothing more."

"Finally," Gram added, her voice softening but no less firm, "you must never remove artifacts that would be missed in their own time."

Eleanor raised a finger, her mischievous smile softening the gravity of the moment. "Except for a few odds and ends. Sometimes we dip into the past for mundane items—things history won't remember, like a set of teacups or a forgotten book. But we never take anything personal or significant. That's a hard rule."

I nodded slowly, the weight of their words settling over me like a heavy quilt. The idea of time travel had seemed fantastical mere moments ago, but now it felt charged with responsibility—layered with rules and consequences I hadn't fully considered.

"Time travel isn't just an adventure," Eleanor said, her tone reverent. "It's a stewardship. When you travel with us, you'll be part of the delicate balance that keeps the fabric of time intact."

Gram leaned back in her chair, her expression softening with a gentle smile. "It's a big job, but it's also a lot of fun. For now, finish your tea and have another cookie. You'll need your energy."

I followed their lead, sipping the last of my chamomile tea and nibbling on a petite lemon tart. The sweetness melted on my tongue, but my thoughts were elsewhere, circling the rules I'd just learned.

As I set down my cup, Eleanor waved her hand with a flourish. In an instant, the crumbs vanished, the cups gleamed as if freshly washed, and the price tags fluttered back to their original positions. The table, once so welcoming with its tea and treats, was now restored to its pristine showroom state.

"Onward," Eleanor declared, her eyes sparkling with excitement. Then, with a wink, she added, "Or perhaps I should say, 'Back ward.'"

I rose, helping Eleanor from her chair. Her hand was cool but steady in mine. "Check the front door, would you, dear?" she asked over her shoulder.

I turned the latch, ensuring the shop was secure, then followed them through the aisles. We passed carefully arranged vignettes, each grouping like a time capsule. Pioneer-era relics—hand-carved rocking chairs, oil lanterns, and patchwork quilts—gave way to the elegance of the Victorian age with its mahogany armoires and intricately patterned rugs. The sleek lines and gilded details of the Roaring Twenties glittered in the soft light, their glamour timeless. It felt like walking through the chapters of a living history book.

Finally, we stopped at the back of the store, where a large oak door loomed like a secret waiting to be told. Its weathered surface bore the marks of time—layers of paint chipped away to reveal a kaleidoscope of faded red, blue, and green. The brass knob, polished by decades of use, gleamed faintly in the dim light.

Eleanor stepped forward, her hand resting lightly on the knob. She turned to me with a wide grin, her excitement almost childlike. "Get ready," she said, throwing the door open with a theatrical flourish. "This is where the magic happens!"

The air shifted as the door swung inward, and I felt it in my chest—a subtle vibration, like a deep hum resonating in the bones.

There was sound, too—soft and melodic, like distant music carried on a breeze. My breath caught, awe and anticipation tangling together in my chest.

Eleanor walked in and gestured for me to follow.

I stepped forward, holding my breath as I crossed the threshold.

Chapter 21

The Portal

I DIDN'T KNOW WHAT I had expected to see behind the old oak door, but it wasn't this. The space looked like an ordinary storeroom. Shelves lined the walls, crammed with vintage china, porcelain dolls, hatboxes, and countless other odds and ends. The faint smell of cedar and old paper filled the air, a mix of forgotten memories and something just beyond comprehension.

"This," Eleanor said, her eyes sparkling with excitement, "is the time-travel portal. It can take you back to any era, any moment in Enchanted Springs' history. But remember, you must not interfere. You're there to observe, not to change."

Gram practically vibrated with excitement. "No matter how many times I go through the portal, this moment never gets old." She chuckled, clearly delighting in her own joke. "Literally, I suppose."

Eleanor's expression shifted to sudden concern. "Oh, my word! We forgot to postdate our wardrobe."

Gram stepped toward the corridor, already assessing the situation. "No worries. I'm sure we can find something in your collection of vintage clothing."

"There's no need," Eleanor said, waving a hand dismissively. "I'll cast a costuming spell. It's quicker."

She cleared her throat and began to chant, her voice steady as ancient words flowed effortlessly from her lips. The spell wove through the air like a tangible force—until she faltered. Her voice caught, and a brief silence hung between us, like a dropped thread in an intricate tapestry.

Gram noticed immediately. Without hesitation, she stepped in, picking up the melody of the spell without missing a beat. Her hands moved with practiced precision, tracing glowing patterns in the air that shimmered faintly before dissolving.

When the spell completed, a soft pulse of magic rippled outward. I felt a tingling vibration as my jeans and t-shirt transformed into a floor-length dress with a high collar. My hair was swept back into an elegant twist, pinned securely as though styled by an invisible hand. Eleanor now wore a flowing black dress with a lace collar, and Gram sported a deep blue gown with an elegant bustle.

Eleanor forced a laugh, waving a hand dismissively as though to brush off the moment. "Thank you for the assistance, Clara. I apologize for that minor hiccup."

"Of course! Think nothing of it. These things happen to the best of us."

I watched the exchange, unease curling in my stomach. Their brief but loaded interaction spoke volumes. Eleanor's misstep wasn't just a momentary lapse—it hinted at something deeper, something she was trying to downplay.

Before I could dwell on it, she moved briskly, pulling an old leather-bound journal from behind a row of antique clocks.

"This is the ledger," she explained, flipping through the thick, yellowed pages. "A record of every time-travel trip taken through the portal. We can't risk crossing paths with ourselves, so we always check this first."

Her finger traced carefully penned dates and destinations. "Ah, here we go—the Founders Festival of 1910. No one from Enchanted Springs has ever traveled back to that particular event."

With our destination set, she tucked the ledger back into its hiding place and motioned for us to join hands. My pulse quickened as I clasped Gram's hand on one side and Eleanor's on the other.

"Ready?" Eleanor asked.

"As ready as I'll ever be," I said, my voice steadier than I felt.

The moment we connected, the world around us dissolved. The storeroom, the scent of cedar, the shelves of forgotten treasures—all of it melted away into a swirling vortex of light and color. My breath hitched as the ground beneath me disappeared, leaving me suspended in a kaleidoscope of stars and streaks of vibrant hues. My body felt like it was stretching and compressing at the same time, as if time itself were reshaping me.

I closed my eyes, the colors behind my eyelids pulsing in time with the whirlwind. My stomach flipped in a mix of exhilaration and nausea, like the rush of a roller coaster's first drop.

Then, as abruptly as it had begun, the motion stopped.

My feet found solid ground, and my eyes flew open to a world bathed in the warm, sepia tones of 1910.

Everything felt sharper, more alive—the scent of fresh wood mingled with faint traces of kerosene, and the muffled chatter of a distant crowd hummed in the air.

Eleanor, steadying herself against a wooden crate, exhaled slowly, her triumphant grin sparkling in the sunlight streaming through the storeroom's plank walls. "Well, well, well," she said, her voice tinged with satisfaction, "I'd say that was quite the smooth journey. Not bad for an old-timer, eh?"

Gram laughed, shaking her head. "Eleanor, my friend, once again, you've stuck the landing. Ten out of ten!"

Eleanor gave a modest shrug, though pride flickered in her expression. "Even after all these years, I've still got it."

I turned in a slow circle, taking in the rows of wooden shelves stacked with burlap sacks, tins of flour and sugar, and glass bottles labeled in elegant script. The air itself seemed thicker, heavier, as if the weight of time pressed around us.

Gram gestured toward the door leading beyond the storeroom. "Come along. We have a festival to see."

My heart pounded as I followed them into the past, excitement and trepidation warring within me. This wasn't just a visit to history—it was a step into the unknown. And no matter how much I told myself we were only here to observe, I couldn't shake the feeling that, just by being here, we were already part of the story.

Chapter 22

The Founders Festival of 1910

I PICKED UP MY pace behind Gram and Eleanor as they scurried out of the storeroom and into the 1910 incarnation of the shop.

What a transformation! It was like stepping into another world—or, more accurately, another time. The walls, freshly painted in a soft cream color, gleamed in the morning sunlight filtering through the windows. The pine floors, polished to a mirror-like shine, added a warmth that felt both welcoming and timeless.

Most strikingly, the shop wasn't an antique store anymore. It had reverted to its original purpose: an old-fashioned general store, brimming with goods for everyday life.

Shelves and drawers lined the walls, meticulously stocked. There were bins of spices, bricks of soap, and bolts of fabric stacked neatly alongside jars of dried beans and preserves. Near the counter, a tempting array of candy glinted in glass jars: peppermint sticks, licorice, rock candy, and lemon drops. The vibrant colors sparkled like jewels in the sunlight.

Elsewhere, burlap sacks of coffee beans sat beside hand-crank grinders and sturdy tin mugs. Porcelain tea sets gleamed on a nearby shelf, each piece painted with delicate floral patterns. Below them, toys were neatly arranged: miniature sailboats, harmonicas, painted dolls, and tiny toy cradles. By the counter, a glass case displayed embroidered handbags, cameo brooches, and necklaces—a small but elegant selection for the town's women.

A shopkeeper—a middle-aged woman with kind eyes and a no-nonsense apron—approached us with a warm smile. "Clara! Eleanor! How nice to see you both. And who's your guest?" She wiped her hands on her apron, a gesture that felt equal parts habit and welcome.

Eleanor nudged me gently forward, resting a hand on my shoulder. "Martha, I'd like you to meet my granddaughter, Marley." Her pride in the introduction was unmistakable.

Martha leaned slightly over the counter, her curiosity evident. "Here for the Founders' Day parade?" she asked, tidying a stack of neatly folded handkerchiefs.

"Of course," Gram replied, her eyes sparkling.

Martha glanced out the window at the clear blue sky. "Well, you picked a beautiful day for it."

As I tried to take in the charm of the shop, the door swung open with a jingle, and a furious-looking woman stormed inside. Her gray hair, pulled into a bun so tight it looked like it might pop, framed a face set in a perpetual scowl.

"Mrs. Snow," she announced, her voice sharp and commanding. "I need a new sugar bowl. I dropped mine, and it shattered. Cheap piece of German porcelain. Surely you can offer me something of higher quality."

Her eyes swept over the shop like a hawk, her expression pinched.

"Of course, Miss Hettie," Martha replied, unbothered by the woman's demeanor. She led Hettie to a shelf of pottery and china, plucking a sugar bowl with effortless grace. It was simple ivory, edged with a swirl of dainty blue flowers.

Martha wrapped the bowl in brown paper and tied it with twine in a motion so fluid it looked like an art form. Hettie paid without a word, snatched the bundle, and stomped out the door without so much as a thank-you.

The door slammed shut behind her, and I turned to Gram and Eleanor. "Was that Hettie Stillson?"

Gram grinned, clearly amused. "It was. How did you guess?"

"She's on the Founders Festival banners downtown," I said, still processing. "She looks angrier in person."

"Oh, she's just having a bad day," Martha quipped with a wry smile. "On good days, she looks even angrier."

That sent us all into a fit of giggles, the tension from Hettie's stormy presence dissolving into lighthearted laughter.

As the laughter faded, a thought occurred to me. "She didn't seem to notice us. Are we invisible here?"

"Not invisible," Gram said, smiling. "Hettie only sees what she wants to see."

Eleanor's tone was more measured. "We're here, but since we're out of our own time, we might shimmer slightly or phase at the edges. It's subtle—barely noticeable—but it's why we had to dress the part."

"So we look like ghosts," I said, only half-joking.

Eleanor tilted her head. "Well, if you're feeling poetic, sure. But let's not spook the locals."

I let my gaze wander as they spoke, marveling at the living history around us. "So this is 1910," I murmured, trying to ground myself. "Who's the president right now?"

"William Howard Taft," Eleanor said with a nostalgic smile, her knowledge of history suddenly feeling less like trivia and more like personal recollection.

"This is incredible," I said, awe creeping into my voice. "We should've brought Sadie. She'd lose her mind over this."

Eleanor and Gram exchanged a knowing look, but before I could press them further, another thought hit me. "Wait. Can my mom do this? Can she time travel, too?"

Gram chuckled. "Of course, dear. She's a Montgomery. It runs in the family."

"So when she's off on sabbatical, she's not just 'off the grid'?" I asked, putting pieces together. "That's why she's so hard to reach?"

"Well," Gram replied, her eyes twinkling. "She is off the grid. Sometimes the grid doesn't exist where she's going—and the Pony Express and telegraphs can be so unreliable."

I opened my mouth to respond, but the distant sound of a marching band warming up floated into the shop, bright and full of energy.

"Well," Gram said, brushing crumbs from her lap. "Shall we? The parade is about to start."

Chapter 23

A Parade of Memories

A S WE STEPPED OUT of the Mercantile onto the 1910 version of Enchanted Spring's Main Street, I knew we were in the same place geographically—but for all intents and purposes, it was a completely different world.

To begin with, the Mercantile building looked brand new. The bricks were in perfect condition, with no signs of chips or tuck-pointing. The plate-glass window was spotless, and the old, weather-worn door gleamed with fresh paint.

The street was alive with sound and color. Bunting and flags hung from every awning, their bright hues dancing in the breeze. Townsfolk moved with an energy that seemed to electrify the air, dressed in the fashions of the early 1900s: women in long dresses with lace-trimmed parasols, and men in waistcoats and bowler hats.

Children darted through the crowd, waving small flags and giggling as they wove between adults. Nearby, a newsstand displayed neatly folded papers, their bold headlines promising the latest from Washington and beyond.

The street itself was a blend of cobblestone and smoother asphalt, a meeting of tradition and progress. Horse-drawn carriages clattered alongside early automobiles, their brass fixtures glinting in the sun. Gas lamps stood like sentinels along the sidewalks, and the air buzzed with the murmur of conversation, and the clop of hooves on stone.

Eleanor guided us to a prime viewing spot just as the parade began. A booming brass band led the way, their uniforms shining and their instruments gleaming. The lively melody seemed to bounce off the buildings, drawing cheers and applause from the crowd.

Behind them marched a small group of Civil War veterans—Northerners who had settled in Florida after the war. Despite the heat, they wore their old uniforms, their chests adorned with medals that told stories of bravery and sacrifice. The crowd applauded warmly, a gesture of respect that brought a lump to my throat.

Next came the bicycle brigade, their penny-farthings towering over the crowd. The riders wore tweed caps and knickerbockers, performing daring stunts that drew gasps and delighted laughter.

Horse-drawn floats followed, each one a masterpiece of flowers, ribbons, and banners. Local farmers displayed bountiful harvests, while seamstresses waved from floats draped in handmade quilts. Children dressed as historical figures waved enthusiastically, their costumes simple but lovingly crafted.

Magnolia University's drama students added a theatrical touch, their Shakespearean costumes a riot of color and texture. Romeo and Juliet performed their lines with dramatic flair, pausing to engage with the audience. Romeo knelt before an elderly woman in the crowd, declaring his love with such passion that she tittered behind her fan, fanning herself dramatically to the delight of her friends.

The energy of the parade was infectious. It wasn't just history brought to life—it was a celebration of the community, a reminder of the people who had built this town with their hands and hearts.

Then I saw him.

At the edge of the crowd stood a bearded man. His wide-brimmed hat cast a shadow over his face, but his sharp, piercing eyes were unmistakable. He wasn't watching the parade. He was watching me.

Recognition hit me like a jolt. Abraham Montgomery—my great-great-grandfather.

I'd seen his face on a Founders Festival banner in my own time, but in person, he was more imposing. His eyes, sharp and knowing, seemed to pierce through me. Did he recognize me? Did he somehow know I didn't belong?

Before I could react, Gram's hand landed firmly on my shoulder, breaking the spell of the moment.

"Come along, dear," she said, her voice calm but her grip steady. She guided me to face the parade. "You're going to want to see this next part."

Her tone was casual, but I caught the flicker of tension in her expression. She'd noticed him too.

"Focus on the parade," she said softly, steering me gently away.

When I glanced back, Abraham was gone, his presence absorbed into the crowd like a shadow dissolving in sunlight.

The rest of the parade passed in a blur. A final marching band brought the festivities to a triumphant close, their brassy notes rising into the blue sky as the crowd erupted in cheers. Eleanor and Gram clapped enthusiastically, their faces alight with the joy of reliving the past.

But my thoughts lingered on Abraham, his intense gaze burned into my memory.

As the crowd began to disperse, Eleanor checked her watch and gestured toward the Mercantile. "We'd better head home," she said.

We made our way back through the Mercantile storage room. Once again, we were surrounded by a swirling vortex of light and energy. As it enveloped us, the hairs on my arms standing on end. The air rippled like the surface of a pond disturbed by a gentle breeze, and then, with a soft whoosh, a swirling kaleidoscope of light enveloped us completely.

The mix of weightlessness and the tug of time weaving around me was less surprising this time. Colors and sounds swirled in the chaos. Moments from the parade flashed through my mind, mingling with fleeting images of Enchanted Springs through the years.

With a gentle jolt, the light receded, and we were back in the present-day storeroom. The familiar scents of cedar and age greeted us, grounding me in the here and now. Gram and Eleanor released their grips on my hands, their smiles warm and satisfied.

"Well, that was quite the adventure," Gram said with a chuckle. "And how about that parade, Marley? Just like the history books, but better."

I nodded, my thoughts still on Abraham Montgomery. "It was incredible," I said, though my voice sounded distant.

Chapter 24

The Grandfather Paradox

T HE HUM OF MODERN life seemed sharper after the quiet of 1910. My thoughts were spinning—and so was my stomach. I leaned against the wall for balance, my breath coming in uneven gasps.

Gram noticed my unease and gently guided me to one of the overstuffed chairs in the corner of the shop. "Sit, dear," she said softly but firmly. "You've had quite the day."

I sank into the chair, but my mind refused to settle. The image of Abraham Montgomery's piercing gaze wouldn't leave me. I had seen his face countless times in photographs and on festival banners, but seeing him—truly seeing him—had been something else entirely.

"Gram," I began hesitantly, "that man at the parade—he was Abraham Montgomery, wasn't he?"

She nodded.

I swallowed. "He was looking right at me. Could he have recognized me?"

Gram sighed, pulling up a chair to sit across from me. Her expression shifted from gentle concern to something heavier. "He might have," she admitted. "There is a strong family resemblance, as you know. That's why I turned you away. Encounters like that are rare, but they can be dangerous."

I leaned forward. "Why? He's my great-great-grandfather, right? Why would it be a problem if he saw me?"

Gram's gaze flickered, and I could tell she was weighing her words. "You've heard of the grandfather paradox, haven't you?"

A cold shiver ran down my spine. "If a time traveler goes back and prevents their own grandfather from meeting their grandmother, they'd never be born.

"Exactly." Gram's voice was steady, but there was something grim beneath it. "But that paradox isn't just a thought experiment—it's a real, terrifying possibility."

A lump formed in my throat. "You think that could happen to me?"

She seemed to choose her words carefully. "I don't know. Time has a way of correcting itself when something disturbs it. If you were to interfere with the choices that led to your own existence..." She trailed off.

My breath hitched. "You mean I could just... cease to exist?"

Gram's lips pressed into a thin line. "I don't think it's that simple." She set her teacup down, eyes dark with thought. "Maybe time would erase you entirely. Or maybe it would unravel you slowly, piece by piece. Your memories might shift. Your body might begin to exist out of sync with the world around you. Or—"

She hesitated, a shadow crossing her face.

"Or what?" I pressed, my pulse hammering.

Her voice was barely above a whisper. "Or maybe time wouldn't erase you at all. Maybe you'd become a paradox—a person who was never supposed to exist. An echo caught between realities."

A cold weight settled in my stomach.

Eleanor patted my arm with a reassuring smile. "Don't let it overwhelm you, dear. Existential doom has a way of sorting itself out."

I blinked at her. "That is not comforting, Eleanor."

She waved a hand airily. "Oh, nonsense. I've been skimming the edges of paradox for decades, and I'm still here—at least for the most part."

Gram ignored Eleanor's antics and focused on me. "Marley, time is fragile. When we travel to the past, we exist outside its natural flow. If someone from that time truly sees us—not just as part of the background, but as something out of place—it disturbs the balance. The past starts to notice. And that's when things spiral."

I exhaled slowly. "Spiral how?"

Gram tilted her head, as if deciding how much she wanted to say. "Think of it like a ripple in a pond. What starts as a small, barely noticeable disturbance can grow into a wave. A single encounter might seem insignificant, but it could lead to questions. Those questions could lead to choices, and choices..."

She met my eyes, her meaning clear. "Choices can rewrite history in ways we can't predict—ways that could erase your present."

I nodded slowly, though the knot in my stomach hadn't entirely eased. "But why did he look at me like that? Do you think he sensed something?"

Gram pursed her lips. "It's possible," she said after a moment. "Abraham was a sharp man, deeply intuitive. Maybe he saw something familiar in you—something he couldn't quite place." She shrugged. "Or maybe it was just coincidence.

I wasn't sure I believed in coincidence anymore.

Gram's expression softened as she reached across to take my hands, her warmth grounding me. "Marley, if something like this happens again, walk away. Do not engage. Do not draw attention to yourself."

I nodded, absorbing her words.

"Remember," she continued, "the past is a place to visit, not a place to belong. Keep your distance, observe, and if you ever feel out of place, lean on me or Eleanor. That's what we're here for."

I took a shaky breath, feeling the weight of her words settle in my chest. "I understand."

Gram squeezed my hand one last time before releasing it. "You'll learn, Marley. This was your first real lesson in time travel—and you passed with flying colors."

Chapter 25

Sadie Meets Eleanor

ELEANOR UNLOCKED THE SHOP'S front door, and not a moment later, Sadie walked in, her tote bag slung over her shoulder.

When Eleanor spotted her, her entire face lit up with delight. "Oh, Sadie! I'm so happy to see you again!" She toddled forward with her arms outstretched like an exuberant grandmother greeting her favorite grandchild.

Sadie hesitated, offering a polite handshake, her academic professionalism firmly intact. "It's a pleasure to meet you, Miss Somerville."

But Eleanor ignored the handshake entirely. Instead, she clasped both of Sadie's hands warmly, her smile wide enough to rival the sunrise. "Oh, Sadie, we've already met! Don't you recognize me?"

Sadie's smile wavered for a moment. She tilted her head slightly, her expression a mix of confusion and apology. "I don't think so."

Eleanor waved her free hand dismissively, laughing as though Sadie had told a joke. "Well, if we haven't met yet in this timeline, we will shortly!" With that, she pulled Sadie into a hug so tight it might have dislodged a lesser woman's ribs. She rocked her gently, murmuring, "It's just so lovely to see you again!"

Over Sadie's shoulder, I caught her wide-eyed look of alarm and the unspoken question etched across her face: *What is happening?*

I could only shrug helplessly, biting back a laugh. It was peak Eleanor, and Sadie was handling it with impressive grace for someone unprepared for such enthusiastic affection.

Finally, Eleanor released her, patting Sadie's cheek fondly. "There now! All settled."

As they stepped apart, Sadie adjusted her tote bag and pulled out a file folder. "I've been researching the history of the Springs Hotel," she began, her tone brisk, "and, well, I've found some interesting facts about Colette Rios, the woman who disappeared without a trace."

We moved to a table in the back of the shop, where Sadie spread out her findings. The atmosphere grew charged with anticipation as she laid out faded newspaper clippings, photocopied documents, and her notes, all illuminated by the soft glow of the overhead lamps.

"Okay," Sadie began, her excitement evident. "I spent hours in the Magnolia University archives, digging through everything I could find on Colette Rios and the history of the hotel." She paused, gesturing to a stack of clippings. "Colette inherited the hotel after her father passed away in 1943. His will made her the sole heir."

I leaned in, scanning the page. "Scarlett mentioned that, didn't she? At Opal Hush."

"For the time, it was unusual," Sadie continued. "Colette was married, but her father's will specifically excluded her husband from inheriting the hotel in the event of her death. He made sure it would stay entirely under Colette's control."

Gram tilted her head thoughtfully. "How did her husband react to that? Was he jealous? Angry? Did that inheritance give him any financial incentive to murder that poor woman?"

Sadie shook her head. "Nope. The husband was excluded completely. If Colette died, the property would have gone to a cousin. So, there wasn't much financial motive there."

"Still," Eleanor murmured, folding her hands in her lap, "if the husband had a wandering eye or a wandering heart, there could have been other reasons for tension. Were there any other suspects?"

Sadie sighed, flipping through her notes. "Not really. There wasn't much of an investigation. Back then, they treated it as a missing person case, not a murder. And as they say, 'no body, no crime.' Plus, Colette had the bad luck to disappear at the end of World War Two. The world's attention was elsewhere."

Gram shook her head sadly. "So her case was lost in the shuffle."

"Exactly. Japan had just surrendered, Germany was in ruins, and the whole world was focused on rebuilding. It wasn't a great time for a local mystery to get attention." Sadie hesitated, then reached for a faded newspaper clipping at the edge of her pile. "But I did find something that might be important."

We all leaned closer, our curiosity piqued.

"According to the archives," Sadie explained, "Colette had planned a grand ceremony to open a time capsule that had been sealed by the hotel's founder in 1920. It was supposed to be the centerpiece of a celebration marking the hotel's twenty-fifth anniversary."

"Interesting," Eleanor said, her brow furrowed.

Sadie nodded. "It was meant to be a big deal—celebrating the hotel's history while sealing a new capsule for future generations. But here's the strange part: Colette disappeared just days before the ceremony. Her absence sparked rumors and concern among the townsfolk."

Gram's face grew thoughtful. "And the time capsule?"

Sadie's eyes gleamed with determination. "That's the thing. The original time capsule was never opened. Or if it was, there's no record of it."

Eleanor leaned back, her expression contemplative. "So you're saying the capsule might still be there at the hotel? Un-opened?"

"Exactly," Sadie said, nodding. "And whatever Colette intended to include in the new capsule is a mystery too. There's no documentation about it after her disappearance."

Gram tapped her chin, her gaze distant. "If we could find the time capsule, they might hold the answers we're looking for. Clues about Colette's disappearance—or even why she was targeted."

I felt a thrill of excitement ripple through me. "Could we really find it? If the time capsule is still hidden at the hotel, it might lead us to something big."

Sadie leaned forward, her voice steady but charged with purpose. "That's what I was thinking. If we can find it, we might be able to uncover something no one else has."

The idea felt both overwhelming and exhilarating. "Then that's our next step," I said, feeling the weight of the mission settle over me. "We find the time capsule."

Chapter 26

Sour Orange Pie

As SADIE PACKED UP her files, Gram's gaze flicked to the antique grandfather clock in the corner. Its hands ticked steadily toward a moment of apparent importance, and her eyes widened in sudden realization.

"Look at the time!" she exclaimed, her voice bursting with urgency, making both Sadie and me jump like startled cats. She grabbed our hands with surprising strength, her grip a force of nature. "We've got pies to bake! Marley, Sadie, I need you both. Every second counts!"

Sadie blinked, her tote bag slipping to the floor. "Pies?" she echoed.

"Pies!" Gram declared, already halfway out the door.

Her infectious energy swept us from the quietude of the antique shop and across the street to the warm bustle of the Enchanted Oven. Gram barreled in like a general readying her troops, flipping on ovens and hauling out mixing bowls, flour, sugar, and what looked like an entire crate of oranges.

"We've got to get our entry into the Founders Festival baking contest," she declared, slipping into her apron with the practiced precision of a surgeon donning scrubs. "Can you imagine if the Enchanted Oven wasn't represented? I'd never live it down."

Before Sadie or I could fully process what was happening, a familiar shimmer caught my eye, and Violet floated into the bakery. Her spectral form was dressed to impress—or at least entertain. She sported a towering chef's hat perched at a jaunty angle, a frilly apron tied at her waist, and—most impressively—matching oven mitts.

"I'm here to help!" Violet announced, striking a pose as though she'd just taken the stage at the Cotton Club.

Gram turned, arching an eyebrow. "Violet, you're a ghost. You can't exactly bake."

Violet waved a dismissive oven-mitted hand. "Pfft. Physical labor was never my strong suit, alive or dead. But I'm an expert cheerleader—and I've been pie-eyed for a century! Nobody knows pie like I do."

I stifled a laugh as Violet twirled dramatically, the chef's hat wobbling precariously.

"Fine," Gram said with mock exasperation, tying her apron strings. "But keep the dramatics to a minimum. We're on a schedule."

"Dramatics? *Moi*?" Violet perched on a stool, her oven-mitted hands folded primly in her lap. She began humming a jaunty Jazz Age tune, swinging her feet like a schoolgirl.

Gram tossed aprons at Sadie and me, her enthusiasm practically glowing. "Let's get to it, ladies!"

"What are we baking?" Sadie asked, catching her apron mid-air.

"Sour orange pies, of course," Gram replied, pulling out a gleaming citrus juicer.

Sadie raised an eyebrow, intrigued. "Sour orange pies? That's not a thing."

"Oh, it's a thing," I said, grinning as I tied my apron. "They're like key lime pies, but better—thanks to the bittersweet oranges that grow around here."

Sadie wrinkled her nose. "You mean those oranges in everyone's yard? I tried one when I first moved here. It was like biting into a lemon dipped in regret."

Gram chuckled, hefting a crate of sour oranges onto the counter. "Exactly. But with the right touch—and a little kitchen magic—you'll see they're a gift from heaven."

As the three of us got to work, the bakery filled with the sharp, zesty scent of fresh oranges. Violet floated around like an overly enthusiastic baking coach, her commentary a blend of encouragement and comedy.

"That zest is just zippy!" she chirped. "More elbow grease, Marley. Channel your inner pastry goddess!"

"Don't let the meringue fall flat!" she added, pointing a translucent oven mitt at Sadie. "Life's too short for flat meringue!"

Sadie, carefully separating egg whites, shot me a look of amused exasperation. "Does she ever run out of commentary?"

"Nope," Gram said, cracking an egg with a practiced hand. "Think of her as a very chatty sous-chef."

The juice, bright and tangy, simmered on the stove with sugar, cornstarch, and butter, transforming into a glossy custard. The smell was divine—a balance of sweet and tart that made my mouth water.

Gram expertly swirled peaks of fluffy meringue onto each pie, her movements swift and sure. "These pies are going to sweep the bake-off," she declared with a satisfied grin. "They'll be talking about these for years."

"And about us!" Violet added, striking another dramatic pose.

Sadie stepped back to admire Gram's handiwork, her green eyes sparkling. "Okay, I'll admit it—these look amazing."

"They taste even better," Gram promised, sliding the pies into the ovens. "These pies are going to be the talk of the Founders Festival bake-off. She turned to us, her cheeks glowing with satisfaction. "Just you wait and see."

We cleaned the kitchen in record time, laughter and the lingering scent of sour orange pies filling the air. Just as we hung our aprons and began to relax, the bell above the bakery door jingled—a sound that lingered oddly, its faint discordance prickling at my senses.

Chapter 27

Man of Mystery

THE MAN WHO STEPPED inside carried himself with quiet authority. Tall and broad-shouldered, he moved with a grace that belied his size, his suit tailored perfectly to his frame. The fabric was elegant yet unassuming, a subtle navy that complemented the sharp angles of his face. His presence seemed to shift the atmosphere in the room, the air taking on a charged stillness.

"Jack Edgewood!" Gram exclaimed, brushing flour from her hands. Her face lit up with a mixture of delight and satisfaction. "Your timing couldn't be better. These two young ladies could use your expertise."

Jack nodded, his gaze sweeping the room with the precision of someone used to reading a scene. When his sharp blue eyes settled on me, my breath hitched. There was something about the way he looked at me—steady, piercing, like he was searching for something just beneath the surface. My pulse quickened, and I fought the urge to fidget under his scrutiny.

"Marley," Gram said, gesturing toward me, "this is Detective Jack Edgewood. Jack, meet my granddaughter."

I stepped forward, offering my hand. "Nice to meet you."

His handshake was firm, the kind that spoke of quiet strength, and his skin was cool against mine. As our hands touched, a ripple of awareness shot through me—a faint but undeniable sensation, like an electric hum that settled deep in my chest.

"Likewise," he said, his voice low and smooth.

"And this," Gram continued, motioning to Sadie, "is Sadie Arragon. She's a professor at Magnolia University, helping Marley dig into some local history."

Jack turned to Sadie, his demeanor polite but reserved. "Professor Arragon," he said, shaking her hand with the same firm grip. "It's a pleasure." His tone carried the faintest hint of something old-fashioned, as though his words had been polished by time itself.

Sadie smiled warmly, though I caught a flicker of curiosity in her eyes as she assessed him. "Nice to meet you, Detective."

A gleeful voice broke the polite tension.

"Well, well, well," Violet drawled, materializing on the counter with a theatrical swing of her ghostly legs. Her chef's hat was gone, replaced by a flapper headband adorned with an oversized feather. "If it isn't Jack Edgewood, Enchanted Springs' man of mystery."

Jack's lips quirked into the faintest smile, and he inclined his head. "Violet." His voice softened, the name rolling off his tongue like an old, familiar tune. "Still finding ways to make an entrance, I see."

Violet grinned, tossing an invisible pearl necklace over her shoulder. "And you're looking less pallid these days. Decided to play nice with the living, have we?"

Jack chuckled, the sound low and resonant. "And you're still stealing the spotlight."

The casual exchange froze me in place. Jack could see Violet. My mind scrambled to process the implications. That small interaction answered one question while raising a dozen more. Who—or what—was Jack Edgewood?

Sadie's eyes darted between Jack and Violet, her brows knitting in confusion. "Wait—you can see her?"

Jack turned to her with a calm nod. "I can. And I assume you're both new to that particular revelation?"

Violet's grin widened as she leaned back, her form glowing faintly. "Oh, Jack here's got a touch of the otherworldly himself. Don't you, handsome?"

"Not the time, Violet," Jack said mildly, though the corners of his mouth twitched.

Still trying to wrap my head around what I was witnessing, I cleared my throat. "Jack," I began, my voice steadier than I felt, "Gram said you might be able to help with Colette Rios's case."

His expression turned thoughtful, the subtle shift in his demeanor commanding attention. "I remember the case," he said, his words deliberate. "Let me review the archives. I might have something useful for you."

Sadie leaned forward, her curiosity visibly piqued. "You know about Colette's disappearance?"

Jack nodded slowly, his gaze turning distant, as if sifting through long-buried memories. "Everyone in town has heard the story, but some of us have dug deeper than the rumors. It's a case that left scars on this town—and maybe some answers, if we know where to look."

Violet clapped her hands together, her excitement palpable. "Oh, this is shaping up to be so much fun! A detective, a historian, and a witch walk into a bakery—sounds like the start of a delightful scandal!"

Jack's smile was faint but genuine. "Let's hope it ends with answers instead of a punchline."

I couldn't help but smile, a flicker of anticipation sparking to life. Between Jack's quiet confidence, Sadie's academic determination, and Violet's chaotic charm, I felt like we might actually be able to uncover the truth about Colette Rios.

Chapter 28

A Solo Trip Back in Time

THE NEXT DAY FOUND me back at the antique shop, having coffee and doughnuts with my new magical mentors.

"Gram, Eleanor," I began, my voice tinged with both eagerness and the kind of impulsive courage that made me question my own sanity. "I've been thinking about everything you've shown me—the magic, the history, the connections. And, well, I've got this idea."

Clara and Eleanor exchanged a glance, the kind of silent communication that spoke of decades of friendship and a shared penchant for mischief. "What's on your mind, dear?" Eleanor asked, her tone gentle but laced with curiosity.

I leaned forward, my enthusiasm bubbling over. "I want to try time travel on my own."

Eleanor tilted her head, intrigued, while Gram's mouth quirked in a half-smile. "A 'quick trip,' you say," Gram echoed, folding her arms. "As if you're talking about running to the corner store."

"In a way, it is," I said with a shrug. "The Springs Hotel is just a few blocks down from the antique shop, and Enchanted Springs has always been a quiet, safe town. What could possibly go wrong?"

Eleanor's brow furrowed. "Quiet and safe, except for the small matter of Colette Rios disappearing without a trace."

"And what if you witness something dangerous?" Gram chimed in, her voice firm. "Or worse—what if you're tempted to step in? The timeline isn't something you can play with, Marley."

I hesitated, their warnings settling uncomfortably in my chest. Could I stand by and watch someone in danger?

The thought made my stomach twist, but I pushed forward. "What are the odds I'd stumble onto the exact moment Colette disappeared? No one knows what happened to her—it's not like I have a map to the past."

Eleanor's lips twitched into a wry smile. "Funny how often the past finds you when you start meddling with time."

"I get it," I said, straightening my spine. "This isn't a decision I'm making lightly. But I'd rather dive into my training than tiptoe around it forever. I've already been to the hotel's past by accident. This time, I'll go with intention—and a plan."

Gram regarded me thoughtfully, her skepticism softened by a hint of pride. "You sound determined."

"I promise I won't break anything," I said, flashing my most innocent grin, a well-practiced tool from years of convincing Gram to bend the rules.

Eleanor chuckled, a warm, indulgent sound. "She's got the spirit, Clara. Sooner or later, we'll have to let her test her wings. Why not now?"

Gram's gaze lingered on me for a moment longer before she nodded. "All right, Marley. We'll prepare you for your 'quick jaunt.' But you can't just pop into 1945 looking like you just stepped out of a yoga class."

"More magic?" I asked, my voice tinged with hope.

"That's always an option," Gram said, sifting through a rack of vintage clothing. "But there's something about wearing authentic pieces. It grounds you in the past, makes you part of it instead of just an observer."

She pulled out a sapphire blue A-line dress, the fabric shimmering faintly in the shop's golden light. "This will do nicely. Very 1940s."

I slipped into the dress, its fit perfect as if it had been made for me. The tailored waist and gently flared skirt hugged my curves in all the right places, transforming me into someone I barely recognized. Gram added a pair of gloves and an elegant feathered hat, securing it with a tilt that felt both fashionable and confident.

"Every detail matters," she said, adjusting the hat with care.

Eleanor bustled over to a jewelry display, returning with a delicate silver charm bracelet. "This will complete the look," she said, clasping it around my wrist.

She traced each charm with her fingertip, her voice reverent. "A sun for enlightenment, a moon for reflection, a star for guidance, a key to unlock secrets, an hourglass for time travel, and a cat—for mystery and a touch of luck."

The moment the bracelet clicked into place, a faint shimmer of magic danced through the air, making my skin tingle.

Before I could comment, Violet materialized, cradling Twila in one arm while chewing a piece of gum with exaggerated flair. She popped a bubble, surveying me like a fashion editor judging a runway show. "Well, well," she said, gesturing for me to twirl. "Let's see the whole look."

I spun once, the hem of the dress swishing dramatically.

Violet clapped her hands, a grin spreading across her ruby-red lips. "You look swell, kid. If I didn't know better, I'd say you were a shoo-in for Miss Enchanted Springs, 1945."

"Thanks, Violet," I said, laughing.

She leaned in conspiratorially, lowering her voice. "Just remember—time travel's like a good Charleston. You've got to hit the right beat, or you'll trip over your own feet."

"I'll keep that in mind," I replied, biting back a smile.

Gram stepped back, surveying me with satisfaction. "Perfect," she declared. "Now, remember the rules: blend in, observe, and don't get involved."

Eleanor nodded. "And if you feel out of place, come straight back. The past has its allure, but it's not where you belong—not yet."

With a deep breath, I looked at my reflection in the shop's antique mirror. Gone was the modern-day Marley. In her place stood a woman who looked like she belonged in the Springs Hotel on its grandest day. The weight of the moment settled over me, equal parts exhilarating and terrifying.

"Ready?" Gram asked, her voice steady.

I met her gaze and nodded, determination coursing through me. "Ready."

Chapter 29

The Springs Hotel, 1945

THE SOLO TRIP TO 1945 was smoother than I'd expected, though the weight of stepping into the past settled over me the moment I emerged from the storeroom. The air carried a heaviness, tinged with the scent of polished wood and the faintest whisper of dust, as if time itself had texture. The sharp clarity of the present was gone, replaced by a softer, golden haze, like the world had been wrapped in the warm glow of an old film reel.

I'd scheduled my arrival for early evening, after the Mercantile was closed. I walked through the shop, slowly, so I could take it all in. Shelves were lined with items that would have been antiques in my time—patriotic pins, tin toys, and paper dolls—now displayed as everyday commodities.

I took a steadying breath, stepped out onto the sidewalk, and locked the front door with the key Eleanor had entrusted to me.

The town I knew had transformed into a tableau of the 1940s. The scent of pipe tobacco and motor oil mingled with the aroma of roasted peanuts from a street vendor. Gleaming automobiles with hulking grilles shared the road with bicyclists and pedestrians. Somewhere, a radio played a tinny rendition of "Boogie Woogie Bugle Boy."

The mix of old and new was everywhere—window displays showcased wartime fashion that balanced practicality with style, while posters on lampposts urged townsfolk to "Buy War Bonds" and "Loose Lips Sink Ships." A uniformed soldier chatted with a girl in a bright floral dress, the laughter between them light but edged with something bittersweet.

The familiar landmarks from my time were dressed in the era's signature details. Window displays featured fashions that blended utility and elegance, while signs boasted goods at prices that felt impossible—ten cents for a soda, twenty-five cents for a haircut. Men tipped their fedoras as they passed women in tailored dresses and pin curls, their conversations punctuated by laughter that seemed brighter, freer.

I walked carefully down the street, trying to look inconspicuous, until I reached the Springs Hotel.

The grand, art deco entrance was just as I'd seen in my earlier time slip—sleek lines, geometric patterns, the subtle luxury of polished brass and frosted glass. The revolving doors gleamed under the light of the marquee, a beacon calling visitors into its embrace. It wasn't just a hotel—it was a stage, a place where people played out moments both mundane and monumental.

I smoothed my dress, adjusted my feathered hat, and stepped inside.

The hum of conversation filled the air, mingling with the soft clink of glasses and the strains of a live piano drifting from the cocktail lounge. The decor was pure art deco—sleek, elegant, timeless. Table lamps with fringed shades cast pools of warm light, adding an air of intimacy despite the room's grandeur.

Crystal chandeliers cast prisms of light onto the black-and-white checkered marble floor. Plush armchairs in deep red and emerald green were arranged in intimate groupings, their curved wooden legs polished to perfection. Along one wall, an ornate bar gleamed with brass fixtures, its mirrored back reflecting bottles of amber and gold. The air was thick with the scent of cigars, perfume, and something decadent—perhaps brandy or the lingering sweetness of a cocktail's sugared rim.

The hum of conversation filled the space, punctuated by the occasional laughter of a guest or the soft clink of glass against glass. A pianist in the cocktail lounge played something smooth and elegant, his fingers drifting effortlessly over the keys.

And then I saw her—Colette Rios. Alive. Vibrant. And obviously unaware of her own fate.

She moved through the room with effortless grace, greeting guests with a nod here, a warm word there. She was perfectly poised, exuding an easy charm that made her seem both approachable and untouchable.

For a moment, I even forgot the tragedy I knew was coming.

In the here and now, Colette Rios was the picture of command and charm. She moved with an effortless grace that turned heads, not because she demanded attention, but because she carried herself like a woman who already had it.

Her cream-colored pencil skirt suit hugged her curves with tailored precision, the pearl buttons catching the chandelier's glow as she gestured animatedly to a guest. Her fiery red hair was swept into an elegant updo, the soft curls at the nape of her neck artfully arranged, not a strand out of place. A single pearl comb nestled in her hair, a delicate contrast to her bold red lipstick. She had the kind of beauty that wasn't just about symmetry—it was about presence. The way she smiled at people, the way her eyes lingered just long enough to make them feel seen.

I was mesmerized.

It was one thing to read about her, to see her ghost flicker in and out of my world. But to watch her now, full of life, completely unaware of the shadow looming over her—it sent a chill down my spine.

Each smile, every gesture, felt laden with meaning. Was there a clue in the way she held herself? A hint of unease beneath her charm?

As Colette paused to exchange pleasantries with a guest, a strikingly handsome man entered the lobby. Dark-haired, with an easy confidence that turned heads, he moved with the assurance of someone used to being noticed. Colette nodded to him, her expression cordial but restrained. He nodded back, a flicker of something unspoken passing between them.

Ricardo Rios. I recognized him, too, from the photo Sadie had found.

Ricardo returned Colette's nod, his lips curving into a slow, knowing smile. There was something unspoken between them, something layered. Tension? Amusement? A history only they understood?

He continued toward the bar, leaving behind a whisper of intrigue in his wake. I followed at a safe distance.

The barmaid straightened as he approached, her cheeks pinkening as she tucked a stray hair behind her ear. "Hello, Ricardo," she said, her voice soft but tinged with nerves. Then, quickly correcting herself: "I mean, Mr. Rios."

He smiled, leaning slightly on the bar as if he had all the time in the world. "Ricardo is fine," he said smoothly, his tone rich and effortless.

I could understand why she had stammered a bit. Ricardo Rios was a good-looking man. Actually, strike that. He was handsome. I wouldn't even be exaggerating to say he was drop-dead gorgeous. He was as suave and debonair as a movie star, with chestnut hair, mesmerizing brown eyes, and a brilliant white smile that revealed a perfectly matched pair of dimples above a sculpted jawline.

He exuded effortless charm in a crisp linen suit, tailored to perfection in a sandy beige that complemented his sun-kissed complexion. His trousers were pressed to perfection, with a sharp crease that elongated his stature. The ensemble was completed with dark leather loafers worn without socks. The full effect almost made me stammer, too.

He glanced around the room, then turned back to Natasha. "How goes everything in the lounge today?"

Natasha stepped back, adjusting her apron, her fingers skimming the fabric as if grounding herself.

"Lively as ever, Ricardo."

I wanted to get closer, to observe without standing out. Slipping into an open seat at the bar, I folded my hands on the polished wood and ordered the first drink that came to mind.

"Could I have an Opal Hush, please?"

Natasha tilted her head, a puzzled smile tugging at her lips. "I'm afraid I don't know that one."

Ugh. I should have known better than to order a specialty drink from my own time. My brain scrambled for a way to recover.

"It's pretty simple," I said quickly, keeping my tone light. "A mix of red wine—claret, if you have it—and carbonated lemonade. The foam creates this shimmering, opalescent glow. It's simple but really beautiful."

Natasha's eyes lit up with intrigue. "That does sound enchanting. Let me give it a try."

She reached for the ingredients with quiet confidence. As she poured the claret, the deep red liquid swirled richly in the glass. Then, using a soda siphon, she carbonated the lemonade and added it in a gentle stream. The drink bubbled to life, creating a frothy, shimmering foam that sparkled faintly under the bar's warm lighting.

"How does that look?" she asked, tilting the glass toward me.

I took it, my fingers brushing against the cool stem. "Perfect."

As I sipped my drink, my gaze wandered across the lounge, taking in the patrons who seemed caught up in their own little dramas. A woman in a green satin dress laughed too brightly at something her companion whispered, while a man in a pinstriped suit shuffled a deck of playing cards with practiced ease, his eyes scanning the room for a worthy opponent.

Alone in a shadowed corner of the bar, a dark-haired man stirred his drink with deliberate slowness, his gaze fixed not on the lively crowd, but on something far beyond it. He was dressed simply—a crisp white shirt, black tie loosened just enough to suggest he'd been sitting there for some time, and a well-cut dark jacket that seemed deliberately unremarkable.

For the briefest moment, his gaze flicked to mine. It wasn't flirtatious, nor was it dismissive. It was assessing. Calculating. Then, as if I had been measured and cataloged, he looked away, lifting his glass to his lips.

Ricardo approached me, his charm practically radiating off him as he navigated through the tables with a casual ease that drew the room's attention. "A new face in our midst," he remarked. "And a lovely one at that."

Chapter 30

A Cuban Sunrise

BEFORE I COULD MUSTER a response, he took my hand in his, pressing a kiss to the back with a gallantry that felt as if it belonged to another era. "I am Ricardo," he introduced himself. "Ricardo Rios, proprietor of this fine establishment."

Flattered, I managed a response. "I'm Marley," I replied, stopping myself before I gave away my last name. I didn't want him to connect me to my great-grandparents, who I knew were living less than a mile away.

He moved closer, his gaze falling on the effervescent drink. "A shimmering cocktail," he mused. "What do you call it?"

"It's an Opal Hush," I said, the words feeling strangely significant as they left my mouth.

Ricardo raised an eyebrow, clearly impressed. "Natasha, could you be so kind as to make another Opal Hush, for me?"

As Natasha prepared a second Opal Hush, Ricardo turned my way again.

"What brings such a charming young lady to Enchanted Springs?" His tone was laced with an interest that bordered on flirtation.

Surprised by his forwardness, I scrambled for an answer that would keep my real purpose hidden. "I have relatives in town," I stammered, hoping my smile hid the flutter of nerves his proximity induced. "So I'm just visiting and taking in the sights."

Natasha handed him an Opal Hush. As he sipped it, he winked at me.

"My darling, I think we've just found our newest signature cocktail. It tastes like the light of a Cuban sunrise."

"Are you from Cuba?" I knew he was, of course, not only because of his accent. Sadie had briefed me on his role in the drama that was now unfolding before my eyes.

Of course, she couldn't have described the melodic lilt of his accent that seemed to carry the warmth of the Caribbean sun. The rhythm of his words was laced with the melody of the island, and he rolled his Rs sensually on the tip of his tongue.

Ricardo's eyes lit up at my question, a spark of genuine pride flickering in them. "Yes, from *Cojímar*, a small village just outside Havana." His voice was tinged with nostalgia. "It's a humble place, but rich in spirit and beauty. The sea there... it's like it knows all our stories."

"And how did a man from Cojímar find his way here to Enchanted Springs?"

A soft smile played on his lips. "Ah, that is a tale of fate and fortune," he began, his gaze drifting momentarily to where Colette oversaw the lobby with an air of regal composure. "I was a fisherman, finding my way as a guide, when I found myself in Miami. A kind man and his daughter hired me for an afternoon outing—and that is how I met my dear, sweet Colette."

He paused, as if the memory held a sacred place in his heart. Then he looked at his wife and smiled with affection.

"She was unlike any woman I had ever encountered—strong, independent, with a vision for her life that was as clear as the waters of my beloved Cojímar. I was captivated, not just by her beauty, but by her spirit."

As Ricardo recounted the tale of their serendipitous meeting, his eyes alight with reminiscence, I couldn't help but feel drawn into the warmth of their story.

At that moment, however, a slight shift in the air caught my attention. It was almost imperceptible, but I could feel a powerful, emotional energy radiating from behind the bar. I subtly turned my attention to the barmaid.

Natasha looked tense, her smile faltering ever so slightly as Ricardo admired his wife. It was a fleeting moment, but in it, I saw a flicker of something raw and unguarded: jealousy.

I offered Natasha a sympathetic glance, an unspoken acknowledgment of the complexity of her feelings, but she was already back to her professional demeanor, attending to another guest with her practiced charm.

I watched as Colette approached the bar. Natasha greeted her with a practiced smile, reaching for a bottle and a glass. "Your usual, Mrs. Rios," she said, her voice light but carrying an undercurrent of something I couldn't quite place.

She moved behind the bar with a grace that belied the tension simmering beneath the surface. Her hands, steady and practiced, reached for the familiar bottles to prepare a gin martini.

I watched, fascinated by the ritual of it. The precise measure of gin, the vermouth's whisper, the gentle stir that chilled the mixture to perfection. Natasha then strained the liquid into a chilled glass, its surface kissed by the cool air. An olive, skewered with meticulous care, completed the drink.

As Natasha placed the martini on a coaster, she slid it across the bar towards Colette with a smile that didn't quite reach her eyes.

Colette offered a nod of appreciation, and as she took a sip, her eyes closed momentarily in pleasure.

I had seen enough to satisfy my curiosity. I finished my drink, paid with the cash that Eleanor had slipped into my purse, and made my way back through the lobby.

As I passed the registration desk, I glanced at the clerk stationed there. He was engrossed in his duties, scanning a ledger with the focus that spoke of a man dedicated to the minutiae of his role.

He must have sensed me watching him, because he looked up. As our eyes met, he offered a nod, his expression one of professional courtesy. "Good afternoon, miss," he said, his voice carrying the crisp, formal tones of a bygone era. "I hope your visit has been pleasant."

"Very much so, thank you," I replied. He nodded once more, then returned to his books. As I stepped through the grand entrance, leaving the cool dimness of the hotel behind, the evening sun outside seemed to cast the world in a stark, new light.

Chapter 31

Ready for My Close-Up

THE RETURN TO MY own time was smooth, almost disappointingly so. I landed on solid ground with no swirling vortex-induced nausea, no temporal whiplash—just a quiet pop as the magic settled around me.

I felt an immediate rush of pride. I had traveled through time—alone. And survived! I was really getting the hang of this time-travel stuff.

I straightened my dress, smoothed my hair, and took a deep, satisfied breath before stepping out of the storeroom, ready to bask in my triumph.

I was expecting the shop to be just as I'd left it—quiet, peaceful, maybe with Eleanor tidying a display case and Gram humming while sorting through inventory.

What I wasn't expecting was absolute, unfiltered chaos.

"Daaaahling! At last, you've returned!"

Violet's voice rang out dramatically as she twirled in place, her spectral form perched in front of an elaborate vanity table that had definitely not been there when I left. The antique mirror was framed in ornate gold, its bulbs flickering with an eerie, otherworldly glow. A vintage phonograph crooned out a sultry jazz tune, setting the mood as powder puffs, lipsticks, and jars of cold cream floated through the air in a flurry of motion, mimicking the beauty routine of an invisible starlet.

My jaw dropped. "Violet, what is all this?"

She gasped, pressing a hand to her heart as if I had just insulted her entire existence. "Marley Montgomery, must you ask the obvious? It's my glamour shoot! The moment history has been waiting for! I'm ready for my close-up, and you, my dear, are my photographer."

I blinked. Then blinked again. "You hijacked the entire shop for a spectral photo shoot?"

Violet waved a translucent hand, as though I were the ridiculous one. "Hijacked? Such an ugly word! I transformed it. Elevated it! Given it the pizzazz this dusty little shop sorely lacks."

My eye twitched as I took in the absurdity of the scene. Where did she even get this stuff? Had she summoned it? Haunted it into existence?

Before I could demand answers, Violet let out a wistful sigh, running an ethereal hand through her bobbed curls. "Imagine it, darling: Violet Serrano, the Ghost with the Most Glamour! Pictorial spread. Center stage. Cover of every supernatural society paper from here to the beyond!" She tossed me a flirtatious wink. "Go on, Marley—immortalize me in pixels."

I groaned, but there was no fighting her when she was like this. "Fine. But you owe me."

"Always," she said smoothly, fluffing her hair with exaggerated grace.

With a resigned sigh, I grabbed my camera from my bag in the storage room. "This isn't something they don't prepare you for in photography school."

Violet grinned. "Oh, but they should!"

She flitted toward the vanity, her ghostly presence casting a faint shimmer against the antique mirror. Then came the "makeup" routine—which, given that she was incorporeal, consisted entirely of enthusiastic miming. A powder puff floated an inch from her cheek, dabbing at air. A lipstick hovered near her lips, never quite touching them. The whole thing was so utterly ridiculous that I couldn't help but burst into laughter.

"Violet, you don't need makeup. You literally glow on your own."

She preened, batting her lashes. "Flatterer! But the show must go on!"

Then came the posing.

One moment, she was the doe-eyed ingénue, chin tilted just so. The next, she was a full-fledged femme fatale, draping herself dramatically over the fainting couch that had also mysteriously appeared.

"Get my good side," she instructed, turning her head at an angle so precise it could have been measured with a protractor. "Though, honestly, I haven't had a bad side since 1923."

I snapped the photo, biting back a snort. "Debatable."

She gasped, clutching her nonexistent pearls. "You wound me, Toots!"

Before I could respond, she suddenly straightened. "Wait! We must include my co-star."

With a flick of her wrist, she summoned Twila, who had been perched on the checkout desk, watching the entire fiasco with the amused detachment of a cat who had seen it all before.

"Twila, this is your moment," Violet crooned, cradling the spectral Siamese like an Academy Award.

I framed the shot, capturing the two of them against the backdrop of the shop's treasures—timeless antiques, much like them. Twila performed a delicate pirouette in Violet's arms, her tail curling in a perfect flourish.

"Was Twila your cat back when you were alive?" The bond between them was so natural, so effortless, that it was hard to believe they hadn't always been together.

Violet laughed, airy and light. "Oh, no, darling. Twila found me here."

She glanced at the kitten, and for the first time, her usual theatrics softened into something gentler.

"I think she sensed I needed someone," she mused, stroking Twila's shimmering fur. "A companion in my afterlife."

Twila blinked lazily, her eyes shifting in color—a mesmerizing blend of sapphire blue, emerald green, and a rich, unnatural violet.

"Look at those eyes," Violet murmured. "They change colors like the twilight sky. That's how she got her name."

I nodded. "They're gorgeous."

Violet nuzzled against her. "She's a little piece of magic, just like this shop. I've always felt at home here, surrounded by reminders of my era. But Twila..." She smiled, nudging the kitten's nose with her own. "She made it more than a sanctuary. She made it a home."

The moment was unexpectedly poignant, and I found myself staring, caught in the simple beauty of it.

Then, as if catching herself being too sentimental, Violet straightened.

"Well, that got emotional," she said with an exaggerated sniff. "Let's wrap this up before I start weeping ectoplasm."

We finished the session with a series of portraits that were equal parts absurd and enchanting. Violet reveled in every moment, her energy never waning.

"Marley, you've done something extraordinary," she said, reviewing the final images. "You've seen us—not just as we appear, but as we truly are. Thank you for seeing into the depths of my soul."

And then, with a cheeky wink, she was gone.

Chapter 32

Suspicious Minds

I CALLED SADIE THE moment I got home, still buzzing from my visit to Colette's hotel. I barely had time to say hello before she launched into full mystery-mode.

"I knew it!" she exclaimed, practically vibrating through the phone. "I kind of suspected her husband. Did you see his photo? That man looked like he could reach out of a five-by-seven print and flirt with us here and now."

I laughed, sinking into my couch with a glass of wine. "I don't need to see the photo. I saw him live and in person."

There was a moment of silence before Sadie let out a dramatic gasp. "Marley. *Marley*. Are you telling me you met the actual Ricardo Rios in the flesh? The same Ricardo Rios whose dimples could disarm a small army?"

I smirked. "In the very charming, very smooth-talking flesh."

Sadie groaned. "Okay, now I'm officially green with envy. That's not fair. You met him. You got to witness that million-dollar smile in action. This is a crime."

I took a sip of wine, relishing the moment. "I mean, I don't want to make you jealous, but he was ridiculously handsome."

Sadie let out a tragic sigh. "I knew it. He was one of those men. The kind who could charm a nun out of her vows."

I snorted. "Oh, definitely. But here's the thing—he really did seem to love Colette."

Sadie scoffed. "Oh, please. Maybe that was just an act. A long con. What if he was planning to murder her for the money and didn't know about the will? And maybe he wasn't working alone. What if he and Natasha were in cahoots?"

The suggestion sent an unexpected chill down my spine.

I frowned, setting my glass down. "You know, I did get the impression Natasha had her eyes on Ricardo."

"Aha!" Sadie crowed. "There it is! The classic 'best friend who's secretly in love with the husband' situation. Or, in this case, the barmaid who's secretly in love with the husband."

My mind drifted back to the way Natasha had poured Colette's drink—her usual, she'd called it. Every day, like clockwork. The pieces of the puzzle started shifting into place, aligning in a way I really didn't like.

I sat up straighter. "Sadie, what if Natasha poisoned her?"

There was a beat of silence. Then, "Oh my god."

"She was the one pouring Colette's drinks. If she was jealous of her—if she wanted Ricardo for herself—it would have been so easy to slip something in." I swallowed hard, hating how plausible it sounded. "And if it was slow-acting, no one would have suspected her right away."

Sadie was eerily quiet for a second. Then, in a hushed voice, she said, "Marley, I actually found something in the archives about Natasha."

I stilled. "What?"

Sadie exhaled, as if steeling herself. "It's the weirdest thing. There are a few mentions of her working at the hotel, serving drinks, chatting with guests. But after Colette vanished? Nothing. It's like she disappeared into thin air."

A cold prickle ran down my spine.

"She vanished?"

"Poof. Gone. No forwarding address, no marriage records, no sign she took another job anywhere. It's like she never existed after 1945."

I stared into my glass of wine, swirling it absently. "So either she ran away, or something happened to her."

Sadie hummed thoughtfully. "Maybe she started over somewhere else. Maybe she had to. Or maybe—"

"She didn't get away with it," I finished grimly.

For a moment, neither of us spoke.

Then Sadie exhaled, shaking off the tension. "Okay, but listen. What if Natasha was in love with Ricardo, and she thought she was helping him by getting rid of Colette? Like, in her head, she thought he'd be grateful?"

I grimaced. "That's honestly kind of terrifying."

"And then when it didn't work out—maybe Ricardo rejected her, maybe he was heartbroken over Colette's disappearance—she panicked and ran."

I shuddered. "It would explain why she dropped off the face of the earth."

Sadie sighed dramatically. "This is all so infuriating. Time travel should make solving murder mysteries easier, but instead, we've just got more questions."

Chapter 33

Cold Case Files

THE NEXT MORNING, MY phone buzzed at precisely seven a.m. I groaned, burrowing deeper into my blankets, but the glowing screen was relentless.

Morning, Marley. I'm in the archives in the basement of the old courthouse. Could you come over? There's something I think you should see.

Jack. Of course he was a morning person.

I rolled onto my back, blinking at the ceiling. Time travel, spectral photoshoots, murder theories—it was a miracle I'd gotten any sleep at all. And yet, here I was, about to drag myself out of bed at an ungodly hour because Detective Mysterious-and-Handsome had found something in the archives.

With a groan, I stretched, tossed on yesterday's clothes and shuffled downstairs. Gram's ever-faithful thermos was filled with black coffee, and I poured two steaming cups before heading out, determined not to show up empty-handed.

The old courthouse loomed over the square, its weathered stone and classical columns exuding an air of quiet authority. The building had stood for over a century, witnessing scandal, justice, and secrets buried beneath layers of history.

The interior was dim and hushed, the sterile marble hallways cool beneath my hurried steps. As I descended into the basement, the air grew heavier, tinged with the faint scent of old paper and something musty, like time itself had settled into the cracks.

A propped-open door led to the archives—a labyrinth of cinderblock walls, metal filing cabinets, and dim desk lamps flickering over stacks of brittle documents.

Jack stood at a long wooden table, sleeves rolled up, tie loosened, his sharp blue eyes scanning a yellowed file with laser focus. The sight of him—disheveled but intensely focused—took me by surprise.

"Good morning, Marley," he greeted, his deep voice warm against the chill of the basement air. "Hope you're ready for this."

I held up the coffee in response. "I refuse to participate in any early-morning sleuthing without caffeine."

His lips quirked into a smirk as he reached for the cup. Our fingers brushed.

A jolt—warm, electric—shot through my arm, tingling up my spine. My breath caught. The air between us shifted, a moment stretching just long enough to make my pulse stutter.

Jack's fingers lingered for half a second too long before he pulled back, his expression briefly unreadable. A flicker of recognition flashed across his face—like he'd felt it too—but just as quickly, his professional mask snapped back into place.

"Let's get started," he said briskly, turning back to the table.

I blinked, shaking off the unexpected charge, and followed him.

"This," Jack began, flipping open a thick, yellowed folder, "is the missing person file on Colette Rios."

The brittle pages fanned out like a long-buried secret being unearthed. A black-and-white photo of Colette stared back at me, her luminous smile frozen in time. It was unsettling, knowing what would eventually happen—or had happened—to her.

"As you can see," Jack continued, "this case was never officially treated as a homicide. Colette vanished, and that was that. The authorities did a cursory investigation, interviewed the usual suspects—her husband, Ricardo; hotel staff; a few guests—but nothing stuck. It was wartime, and people disappeared all the time. No body, no crime."

He gestured toward another photograph.

"Ricardo Rios," he said.

I studied the image, already familiar with his devastating good looks. Even in a grainy black-and-white still, Ricardo exuded effortless charm.

Jack must've caught my expression, because his smile returned, just slightly. "Judging by your face, I assume you understand why he was a person of interest?"

I coughed, schooling my features. "Let's just say he looks memorable."

Jack's smile faded, his expression sharpening. "Memorable, and rumored to have a wandering eye." He pulled out another page, covered in scribbled notes. "The barmaid, Natasha? She was a subject of gossip, too."

I frowned. "Natasha?"

Jack nodded. "There were whispers. That she and Ricardo were too close. That she had her own ambitions. Maybe even her own motive."

A chill prickled along my arms. "What kind of motive?"

Jack tapped a note in the file: the Greek.

I leaned in. "Who's this?"

Jack exhaled slowly. "A mystery guest at the hotel. No full name, just that alias. Supposedly, he was involved in gambling, debts, and some very shady dealings." He hesitated. "There was speculation that Colette knew something she shouldn't have."

A cold unease settled in my stomach. "So you think Colette didn't just disappear. She was silenced?"

Jack's voice was measured, but his gaze was unreadable. "I think there were a lot of people who benefitted from her being gone."

My mind spun with the possibilities—Ricardo, Natasha, the Greek. Who was guilty? Were they all guilty?

Then Jack slid one last document across the table.

"Here's something no one could've known back then," he said.

I picked it up, scanning the page—and froze.

"Wait... what?"

Jack nodded, his expression serious. "Ricardo and Colette were never legally married. Ricardo was already married in Cuba."

My jaw dropped. "Are you kidding me?"

"Not even a little."

My pulse pounded. "So—he had no claim to the hotel? To anything Colette owned?"

"Legally, nothing." Jack's voice was calm, but there was an edge to it. "If he had planned to inherit the hotel through her—well, he couldn't. And if he did know about the will excluding him..." He trailed off.

My thoughts were a whirlwind. "If Colette disappeared, he lost everything?"

Jack nodded. "Which raises the question—did he disappear voluntarily... or did someone else make him disappear, too?"

I exhaled sharply. "And what about 'The Greek'?"

Jack leaned forward slightly, his expression unreadable. "Ah, 'The Greek.' No records. No real name. Just a nickname scrawled in the margins. But there were rumors about him... about gambling debts. And about a motive for wanting Colette out of the way."

A fresh wave of unease settled over me.

This mystery was bigger than I'd realized.

I turned back to Jack, who was watching me with an expression I couldn't quite place.

"You seem to know a lot about this case," I said carefully. "More than someone just reading an old file should."

Jack met my gaze, something unreadable flickering in his eyes. "Go ahead and ask."

The question sat on the tip of my tongue, absurd even as I spoke it.

"Jack... are you a time traveler?"

He didn't answer immediately. He just looked at me. Really looked at me. And for the first time, I had the sinking suspicion that maybe—just maybe—he wasn't only Detective Jack Edgewood.

Maybe he was something more.

Chapter 34

A Man, Not a Monster

J ACK THREW BACK HIS head and laughed, a rich, full-throated sound that echoed through the dimly lit records room. It wasn't the reaction I'd expected, and it sent a jolt of panic through me.

I'd just made a huge mistake. The kind of mistake that could make my grandmother disown me.

My heart pounded. I had just outed myself as a time traveler. To a detective. To someone who could ruin everything.

I scrambled for a way to backtrack. "I was kidding," I blurted, waving my hands like that would somehow erase my words from existence. "Obviously! Just a joke! With all this talk of disappearances and hidden secrets, I thought, 'Hey, let's lighten the mood!'"

Jack's laughter faded as quickly as it had come, and his expression shifted. He studied me with those piercing blue eyes, something unreadable flickering beneath their depths.

"No, Marley," he said, his voice lowering to something quieter. Something heavier. "I know you're a time traveler."

My stomach dropped.

"What?" My voice barely came out.

Jack exhaled, shaking his head with something like awe. "I just can't believe your grandmother didn't tell you who I really am. I have to say I'm impressed, though. She's truly a woman of integrity."

I stared at him. "What are you talking about?"

Jack leaned forward slightly, lowering his voice even though we were alone. "Your grandmother and Eleanor know my story. Because I've been a part of Enchanted Springs for a very long time."

I swallowed hard. "How long are we talking?"

Jack hesitated, his jaw tightening, then sighed. "I'm not a witch. Or a warlock. Or a ghost—before you ask. I am, however, something... not quite human."

I stiffened. "Not quite human?"

Jack smiled faintly, but it wasn't humor. It was something old. Something tired.

"You might be more familiar with the term vampire," he said.

For a moment, my brain completely shut down.

I stared at him, waiting for the punchline. It didn't come.

Jack just watched me, his expression open, expectant.

I forced a laugh, but it sounded strangled. "Okay, sure. Right. You're a vampire. And I'm the Queen of England."

Jack tilted his head slightly, as if considering that. "You do have a certain regal quality."

I scowled. "This is not funny."

He smirked, but only briefly. "No, it's not. But it's true."

A strange tension coiled in my stomach, my mind racing. Time travel, ghosts, magic—I had accepted all of that. But vampires?

Jack must have sensed my internal meltdown because he softened. "I promise, I'm not about to sprout fangs and go all Nosferatu on you."

I crossed my arms, trying to steady my breathing. "You're seriously telling me you drink blood?"

His lips quirked up at the corners. "I prefer refined dining experiences."

"Jack." My voice was sharp.

His smirk faded. "It's complicated. I'm not the kind of monster you're thinking of, Marley. I don't hunt people. I don't skulk in the shadows, preying on innocents." He paused, his voice dipping into something raw. "But I have lived far longer than I should."

I swallowed hard. "How long?"

He hesitated, then murmured, "Around a hundred and fifty years—but who's counting?"

I felt my knees wobble. I staggered back, gripping the edge of the table for support. "Oh my God."

Jack took a careful step forward, his hands up, as if I were a startled animal he didn't want to scare off. "Marley, I told you this because I want you to trust me. You need to know who you're working with."

I stared at him, my head spinning. "Working with?"

Jack exhaled slowly. "Colette's case isn't just history for me. It's personal. I knew her."

My breath caught. "You knew her?"

His gaze flickered with something dark. "Not well. But well enough to know she didn't deserve what happened."

The weight of his words settled over me.

I believed him.

And I hated that I believed him.

Jack Edgewood—Detective Edgewood—was an actual vampire. And, apparently, my partner in solving a cold case from long before I was born.

I sucked in a deep breath, squared my shoulders, and somehow found my voice. "Okay," I said, steadying myself. "So you're a vampire. A preternatural being. Whatever. That's just another weird part of this town I'll have to deal with."

Jack blinked. "You're shockingly calm about this."

I huffed. "Jack, in the last week, I've traveled through time, discovered I can see ghosts, and watched a spectral flapper throw herself a fashion shoot. You being a vampire is, like, fourth on my list of weird things right now."

His slow smile sent something traitorous fluttering in my stomach.

"I like you, Marley Montgomery."

I scoffed. "That's convenient. Because I have so many questions for you."

Jack's eyes glinted. "That's a promise I'm happy to keep."

Chapter 35

Preternaturally Yours

I SMILED, DECIDING THAT if I could be a witch, there was no reason in the world I couldn't be friends with a vampire.

I mean, a preternatural. Might as well be polite and use the term he preferred.

Leaning forward in my seat, I lifted my chin toward the file box. "Was there anything in the records about a time capsule?"

Jack's brow furrowed slightly as he reached into the box and retrieved a particularly worn folder. "As a matter of fact, there was. I didn't think much of it at the time. Why do you ask?"

My fingers brushed against the brittle pages as I opened the folder. There it was—a passing reference to a time capsule that the hotel staff had intended to bury in the attic during the grand opening. I frowned. That wasn't what Sadie had said. Her research suggested it was supposed to be hidden in the cornerstone.

The note was brief, almost an afterthought scrawled in the margins of a witness statement about Colette's disappearance. But its implications sent a thrill of curiosity through me.

"Sadie thought it might be a clue everyone overlooked," I explained, tapping the entry.

Jack leaned back, rubbing his chin thoughtfully. "It's possible. Time capsules are like letters to the future. If the staff included something about Colette—or anything that sheds light on her disappearance—it could be a significant lead."

"We should go look for it."

Jack's head snapped up. "What?"

"We should find it," I pressed. "Let's go to the hotel and see if we can unearth the time capsule."

Jack's expression immediately shifted into what I was starting to recognize as his I'm a responsible adult, and you're trying to rope me into something questionable face.

"Marley," he said slowly, "I can't just start prying into the hotel's structure without permission. Not without a warrant. I am still an officer of the law, and there are—"

"Jack," I interrupted, "this isn't a current crime. This mystery is decades old. We're not breaking into anyone's private space. If the capsule was meant for future generations, then technically, we're just doing exactly what they intended—finding it."

He exhaled, his jaw tightening.

"And," I added, sensing him wavering, "we're just looking at the cornerstone, which is in plain sight. I'm pretty sure there's no law against observing a big block of engraved stone on a public street."

Jack drummed his fingers against the table, eyes locked on mine like he was measuring my level of troublemaking. Finally, he sighed, the corners of his mouth twitching. "You really don't like being told no, do you?"

I beamed. "Not when I have a perfectly reasonable plan."

"This is not a reasonable plan," he muttered, but he was already grabbing his jacket.

I took that as a victory.

The Springs Hotel loomed ahead, its art deco facade glowing under the midday sun. Jack and I approached the engraved cornerstone, its inscription marking the building's grand opening in 1920.

Jack crouched first, running his fingers over the surface with a detective's precision. I followed suit, tracing the stone, searching for any imperfection or clue.

"It would need to be accessible yet concealed," Jack murmured. "Possibly a pressure-activated panel or a hidden latch."

I rolled my eyes. "You're watching too many noir films."

Jack shot me a look. "Marley, I was around during the noir era."

Fair point.

I pressed my hands along the edges of the stone, searching for anything loose. "It could be as simple as a sliding panel," I suggested. "Or maybe there's a—wait. Jack, here."

Jack leaned over as I guided his hand to a barely perceptible notch hidden in the decorative engraving. The warmth of his fingers brushing against mine sent an unexpected jolt through me—not the magic kind. The annoyingly attractive detective kind.

"Feels like a catch," Jack murmured, completely oblivious to my not-at-all-professional reaction to his proximity.

With a soft click, the stone shifted slightly. My breath caught.

Jack carefully wedged his fingers into the narrow opening and pulled. The stone gave way, revealing a hollow space behind it.

We both leaned in, anticipation thrumming through the air.

And found... nothing.

Just an empty compartment.

My heart sank.

Jack exhaled sharply. "Well. That's anticlimactic."

I sat back on my heels, disappointment settling in. "It's empty."

Jack straightened, brushing dust from his hands. "If it was here, someone found it before we did."

I bit my lip. "Do you think it was ever here?"

Jack considered that. "In theory, it was supposed to be." He hesitated. "But you said Sadie thought it was in the cornerstone. The note in the witness statement said attic."

I groaned. "So either the plans changed before the grand opening, or..."

"Or someone moved it," Jack finished grimly.

We stood in silence, the weight of the dead end pressing down on us.

Jack sighed, running a hand through his hair. "This is a bust, Marley. And I need to get back to work. Without concrete evidence or a warrant, I'm already pushing my limits here."

I nodded reluctantly, watching as he walked away, his figure a mix of determination and frustration.

But as the silence settled around me, a new resolve hardened in my chest.

This wasn't the end. It was just a detour.

Chapter 36

Dinner Plans

THE MOMENT JACK LEFT, I pulled out my phone and called Sadie, pacing the sidewalk in front of the hotel. She answered on the first ring. I gave her the condensed version of my morning with Jack.

"I can't wait to see those files for myself," she said. "Do you think he'll give me copies?"

"Probably. But listen. I'm calling from the Springs. Jack and I found the cornerstone, but it was empty. No time capsule. Just an empty hole in the wall."

Sadie hummed thoughtfully. "If it's not in the cornerstone, maybe we need to think outside the box. What about the attic or the basement? If someone moved it, those would be the likeliest places. The attic for sentimental storage, the basement for things people wanted to forget."

"You think we should go look now?"

"Not without me," Sadie said firmly. "There's history in those places, but they're not always safe history. Let's meet tonight. We'll go in after dark."

I bit my lip. "Scarlett's going to kill us if she finds out."

"Which is why we won't tell her," Sadie said brightly. "And if we do get caught, we'll just beg for forgiveness. Easier than asking permission."

"That's your plan?"

"Scarlett likes you. Worst case scenario? We apologize, act very, very sorry, and bring her a peace offering from Gram's bakery."

I sighed. "She does have a weakness for lemon tarts."

"Exactly. Now, let's meet at Opal Hush for dinner. If we're about to sneak into a haunted hotel, we should at least have a decent meal beforehand."

Opal Hush was the perfect place to plot an illegal—technically speaking—midnight exploration.

The evening air was cool and carried a faint dampness as we approached the Springs Hotel. Its silhouette against the night sky was imposing, every shadow and angle hinting at secrets tucked away in its depths. The grand building loomed over us, its facade dimly lit by antique streetlights that cast long, wavering shadows on the cobblestone street.

"Why does it feel like we're walking into a haunted house?" Sadie murmured, her voice barely audible over the faint rustle of leaves in the breeze.

I glanced at her, a mix of nerves and excitement tingling at the edge of my senses. "Maybe because we're about to dive into its underbelly," I replied. "Let's hope the ghosts are in a helpful mood tonight."

We made our way to the dining area. The soft clink of glasses, the warm glow of candlelight, and the low murmur of conversation provided an odd but comforting contrast to our whispered scheming. A jazz trio played in the corner, their smooth melodies adding a soundtrack to our impending trespassing.

Sadie twirled her wine glass between her fingers, her lips curving into a mischievous smile. "So, just to be clear, our plan is to sneak into a historic hotel, rifle through its attic and basement, and hope we don't get arrested for breaking and entering?"

I speared a bite of asparagus risotto. "It sounds reckless when you say it like that."

"That's because it is reckless," she said, grinning.

I sighed dramatically. "Technically, we're not breaking anything. We'll just be... entering in a highly unauthorized manner."

Sadie lifted her glass in a toast. "To bending the law in the name of historical research."

We clinked glasses, and I couldn't help but laugh.

"Scarlett really is going to kill us," I admitted.

Sadie shrugged. "Which is why we'll be charming, apologetic, and bearing pastries."

"You're banking a lot on the power of sugar."

"It's never failed me yet."

We lingered over our meal, stretching out the final bites of lamb chops and risotto. There was something oddly comforting about planning a heist over fine dining, like we were sophisticated art thieves instead of two women with questionable decision-making skills.

Finally, Sadie checked her watch. "It's late enough. Scarlett should be gone by now, and the staff will be focused on closing up."

I took a deep breath, letting the weight of what we were about to do settle over me. "You ready?"

Sadie grinned, tossing back the last sip of her wine. "Always."

Chapter 37

The Basement

W E SLIPPED THROUGH THE hotel's lobby, keeping close to the shadows as if we belonged there. The soft glow of the chandelier above cast elegant patterns on the marble floor, and the faint murmur of conversation from the cocktail lounge drifted toward us. A few guests lingered in the armchairs, too lost in their own evening affairs to pay us any mind.

"This is either a brilliant idea or the beginning of a cautionary tale," Sadie whispered as we approached a discreet corridor near the back of the hotel.

I shot her a look. "If we get caught, we'll just say we got lost looking for the restroom."

Sadie smirked. "Because nothing says 'ladies room' like a staircase to an abandoned basement."

We reached the heavy, wrought-iron staircase spiraling downward into darkness. A tarnished brass plaque beside it read Employees Only. The air that drifted up was cool, damp, and carried the unmistakable scent of aged wood, mildew, and a faint undercurrent of something metallic.

Sadie hesitated, gripping the railing. "Ever notice how nothing good happens in old basements?"

"Yeah, but where better to find buried secrets?"

With that, I pulled open the heavy wooden door and stepped inside.

The metal stairs creaked under our careful steps as we descended, the sound swallowed by the stillness around us. The dim glow from Sadie's illumination spell flickered against the walls, casting long, distorted shadows that slithered like living things.

"Officially regretting this," Sadie muttered.

"Too late now."

We reached the bottom, where a heavy wooden door stood before us, its surface scarred with deep scratches, as though something—or someone—had tried to claw their way out. A chill prickled down my spine.

"Let's hope we find more answers than trouble," I said, pressing my palm against the door.

It groaned as it swung open, revealing the cavernous basement beyond.

The room stretched out in eerie silence, framed by crumbling brick walls and thick wooden beams. The floor was packed dirt, uneven and damp, and the ceiling was low enough that the hanging lightbulbs swayed slightly with each breath of moving air.

Sadie wrinkled her nose. "What is that smell? Like wet socks and regret."

I shrugged. "Welcome to the underbelly of history."

The basement was cluttered with relics of decades past. Dusty crates and rusted metal tools were piled against the walls. Old furniture—chairs missing legs, a warped desk with its drawers yanked out—stood like forgotten sentinels. A massive boiler loomed in one corner, its pipes winding upward like skeletal limbs.

"This is charming," Sadie muttered. "Really cozy."

We split up, moving carefully through the debris, scanning the room for anything that looked remotely like a time capsule. The faint sound of dripping water echoed through the space, each drop amplifying the weight of the silence around us.

And then I felt it.

The air shifted, dropping in temperature so quickly that my breath turned visible. A prickle of unease skittered up my spine. Sadie stiffened beside me, her fingers twitching toward her pocket as if she wished she'd brought something to defend herself.

A voice purred from the shadows. "Well, well, what do we have here?"

I spun, my heart lodging in my throat.

She was leaning against a stack of crates, half in shadow. Natasha.

Her translucent form flickered at the edges, the way old film wavers just before it burns through the reel. Dressed in her crisp 1940s uniform, she looked like a perfectly ordinary barmaid—except for the way her eyes gleamed too brightly in the dim light, reflecting back at me like twin glass marbles.

"Poking around where you don't belong?" she mused, tilting her head just a little too far, like a broken doll.

Sadie inhaled sharply. "Oh, no. Absolutely not."

I swallowed hard and forced my voice to stay even. "Natasha, we're looking for a time capsule. Do you know where it is?"

She smirked, her lips curling in amusement. "If I did, don't you think I would've found it already?" She lifted one hand, her fingers tracing lazy circles in the air. "Believe me, there's nothing down here but dust, regrets, and things that should stay buried."

I frowned. "Why should we believe you?"

Natasha's expression sharpened. "Oh, you shouldn't."

The room dimmed as if the air itself thickened. The shadows deepened, creeping toward us along the floorboards. My pulse kicked up.

Sadie took a step back. "So... this was fun. Let's go."

But Natasha wasn't done. She pushed off the crates, her form flickering unnervingly as she glided forward, stopping just inches from my face.

"You're different," she murmured, her voice almost curious. "You don't belong to my time, but you carry it with you." She inhaled deeply, as though scenting the air. "Magic."

A slow, unsettling smile spread across her lips.

I didn't breathe.

Then, just as suddenly, she vanished, dissolving into the shadows like she had never been there at all.

The silence that followed was deafening.

Sadie exhaled sharply. "That was horrifying."

I nodded, trying to steady my heart. "She'sdifferent from the other ghosts."

"Yeah," Sadie said, still staring at the spot where Natasha had disappeared. "Most ghosts don't smell you like you're a snack."

A shudder ran through me, but I pushed it aside. "She was trying to scare us off."

"Well, congratulations, mission accomplished."

I forced my legs to move, shaking off the tension. "Come on. We're not giving up yet."

Sadie groaned but followed. We resumed searching, sifting through old trunks and crates, checking the walls for hidden compartments. Time stretched, minutes turning into an hour.

Finally, Sadie leaned against a stack of old ledgers and sighed. "I hate to admit it, but Natasha might be right. There's nothing down here."

Frustration prickled at the edges of my patience. I swept my gaze over the space one last time, but the basement only stared back in silent mockery.

"Then we try the attic," I said firmly. "If the time capsules isn't buried, maybe it's hidden upstairs."

Sadie groaned again but pushed off the crate. "Fine. But if we run into another creepy monster ghost, I'm charging you a trauma tax."

"Duly noted."

Together, we climbed the stairs, leaving the damp, oppressive basement behind.

But as we ascended, Natasha's words lingered in my mind: There are things that should stay buried.

For the first time, I wondered if she meant the time capsule—or something else entirely.

Chapter 38

The Attic

THE JOURNEY TO THE attic felt longer than it should have. After a silent ride in the elevator to the top floor, Sadie and I stepped into a dimly lit stairwell that led to a locked door. The air grew warmer as we ascended, the shadows stretching and shifting, as if something unseen stirred just beyond our reach.

Sadie's whispered incantation made quick work of the lock, and with a slow, creaking groan, the door swung open.

Moonlight filtered weakly through grime-covered windows, casting pale beams across the room. The attic was a cavern of forgotten time, where dust settled thickly over generations of memories. It wasn't just a storage space—it was a mausoleum for the past. Every item, every box, every broken chair was steeped in history, waiting for someone to remember.

"This whole attic is a time capsule," Sadie murmured, her voice barely above a whisper.

Unlike the basement, which had been stark and eerie, the attic was suffocating in its stillness. The clutter felt deliberate, as if someone had once tried to preserve these things but abandoned the effort. Stacks of hatboxes, suitcases, and old trunks loomed around us, their lids slightly ajar, revealing glimpses of bygone lives. Gilt-framed mirrors leaned against the walls, their surfaces clouded and dull, reflecting only warped, distorted versions of ourselves.

A headless mannequin stood in one corner, draped in a moth-eaten evening gown. An overturned phonograph sat on a wooden crate, its needle frozen mid-song. A child's rocking horse with chipped paint rested near a stack of discarded ledgers, as if waiting for a child who would never return.

As we navigated the labyrinth of forgotten things, the wooden floorboards groaned beneath our feet, the sound echoing like a whisper of protest.

Then, out of the corner of my eye, I saw movement.

My breath caught as I turned. Seated at an old rolltop desk was the desk clerk I'd seen in 1945.

He hadn't changed much. His face was still careworn, but his spectral form crisp and detailed, as if his spirit had found a place where it felt most at home. The desk was cluttered with ledgers and paperwork, an ink bottle and pen poised as though waiting for a hand to take them up again.

He didn't look up right away. Instead, he ran his fingers through the pages of an old ledger, his expression lost in memory.

For a moment, he didn't seem to notice us. He dipped a fountain pen into an inkwell and scribbled something in the record book. His movements were smooth and practiced, as if he had done this a thousand times before. Then, without looking up, he spoke.

"Welcome to the Springs Hotel," he said, his voice warm and polite, tinged with a formality that felt both practiced and deeply ingrained. "Do you have a reservation?"

Sadie and I exchanged startled glances. He sounded like he was still on duty, still part of the living world.

I swallowed hard. "Sorry, no. But we're not looking for a room."

He finally looked up, adjusting his glasses as his gaze settled on me. He studied me for a long moment, something like recognition flickering across his face.

"My apologies," he said smoothly, rising from his chair. He straightened his vest, brushing away nonexistent dust, and nodded politely. "Irwin Foster, at your service."

I took a careful step forward. "Irwin," I said gently, "do you realize you're in the attic?"

He blinked slowly, as if waking from a dream. His eyes drifted around the room, taking in the decay, the cobwebs, the dust.

"Ah," he murmured, his voice tinged with melancholy. "So I am."

He let out a sigh, straightening the lapels of his jacket. "You'll have to excuse me. I must have lost myself for a moment."

Sadie and I exchanged a glance. There was something heartbreakingly human in the way he tried to compose himself, smoothing the wrinkles of a uniform that had long since faded from the world.

He closed the spectral ledger in front of him and stood, adjusting his tie with meticulous care. "Time has a way of slipping through my fingers these days," he admitted. "And yet, I remain. The guests have gone, the music has stopped, but here I am."

"You've been waiting for something," I said gently.

Irwin gave a wistful smile. "For someone," he said. "Someone to listen. Someone to remember."

A silence stretched between us, thick with the weight of things left unsaid.

"We've heard the rumors," Sadie said, stepping forward. "They said you ran off with Colette."

Irwin let out a short, humorless laugh. "Yes. People do love their stories, don't they?"

He shook his head, his expression distant. "Rumors painted me as Colette's secret lover. A scandalous affair. A man caught between passion and duty." He smiled wistfully. "Flattering, perhaps, but wholly untrue. Colette was out of my league. And to be honest, I worried I was the butt of a joke."

He pressed his palm against the desk, his ghostly fingers passing through the wood. "But when Colette disappeared, the laughter turned to suspicion, and my world crumbled. The hotel closed.

My livelihood vanished, and with it, my purpose. I wandered, lost, until death claimed me. And then, I found myself here, back within these walls, waiting for a chance to clear my name."

His voice, though steady, carried the weight of decades of loneliness.

"We'll help you," I promised, my chest tightening at the sheer isolation of his existence. "We'll find the truth."

Irwin's spectral form flickered slightly, as if the weight of gratitude made him more solid. "Thank you," he said, and for the first time, his voice carried something other than sorrow. "Even the dead deserve the truth."

I hesitated before asking my next question. "Irwin, why is Natasha still here?"

His expression darkened. "Natasha?"

"She's in the basement," Sadie said. "And she's... different."

Irwin's brow furrowed, and his translucent form wavered slightly. "I should have known she wouldn't move on," he murmured. "Natasha had her own ghosts, long before she became one."

"What do you mean?" I asked.

"Natasha knew more about this hotel than anyone. She saw things, heard things that others ignored."

He exhaled, a habit left over from life. "When Colette vanished, Natasha was never the same. Guilt clung to her, like she knew something but couldn't speak it aloud. She believed that if she just found the right clue, if she could unearth whatever truth had been buried, she could make things right."

"But she never found it," Sadie murmured.

"No," Irwin confirmed, his voice heavy with regret. "And so, I suspect, she remains—like me, caught between hope and despair."

Sadie reached for my hand, her grip warm and grounding. "We'll help her too," she said quietly.

Irwin nodded, his form flickering slightly. "But for now, how may I assist you?"

"We're looking for the hotel's old time capsule," I said. "Do you know where it might be?"

His eyes brightened. "The time capsule! Of course. It was meant to be part of Colette's celebration, but after everything happened, it was forgotten. Follow me."

Irwin led us through the attic, his form gliding effortlessly between the stacks of forgotten belongings. Finally, he stopped beside a high shelf, pointing to a dusty metal cylinder hidden behind old boxes.

"There it is," he said, his voice tinged with satisfaction.

Sadie beamed a light toward the shelf, and I carefully retrieved the capsule, my hands trembling slightly as I brought it down. The cool metal was heavy with the weight of history, its surface etched with the passage of time.

"Thank you, Irwin," I said, turning to him with genuine gratitude.

He smiled. "I'm glad I could help. There's so much about this hotel, about this town, that shouldn't be forgotten."

As we left the attic, the shadows seemed to shift, Irwin's figure fading into the gloom. I couldn't shake the feeling that, in some small way, we had begun to unravel the web of stories that bound the Springs Hotel to its past.

And, just maybe, we had given Irwin the first step toward finding his way home.

Chapter 39

The Time Capsule

IN THE QUIET OF Sadie's small kitchen, with the metal time capsule resting on her vintage Formica table, Sadie and I exchanged a glance. The moment crackled with energy, like a held breath waiting to be exhaled. This wasn't just a historical find—it was a message from the past, a whisper truth at long last.

"Are you ready for this?" Sadie asked, her fingers hovering over the lid.

I nodded, my pulse quickening. "Absolutely."

With the kind of care usually reserved for ancient relics, she unlatched the capsule and slowly lifted the lid. A soft sigh of air escaped, as if the past itself had been waiting to be set free.

Inside, layers of delicately folded cloth protected its contents. We unwrapped them carefully, peeling back time one fabric layer at a time.

The first thing we found was a stack of black-and-white photographs, their edges worn but their images remarkably crisp. We spread them out across the table, both of us leaning in as if drawn into the captured moments.

Colette, radiant and full of life, stood at the center of nearly every photo. In one, she held a champagne flute high, laughing amidst elegantly dressed guests. In another, she stood in the grand ballroom, directing staff as they arranged tables for a gala. There were candid shots, too—Colette perched on the check-in desk, kicking her heels playfully as she chatted with a bellboy, or sipping a cocktail at the bar with a mischievous smirk. She wasn't just the hotel's owner; she was its heart.

Beneath the photos lay a bundle of letters tied with a faded blue ribbon. The pages, yellowed but still sturdy, were filled with elegant handwriting. As we carefully unfolded the first one, the words leapt off the page, alive with personality.

My Dearest Friends: The Springs Hotel is more than bricks and chandeliers. It's a promise, a home for dreamers and wanderers alike. I can only hope the future is kind to it.

I swallowed hard. "She knew. She knew how special this place was."

Sadie's voice was hushed with awe. "And she wanted to make sure people remembered."

We continued our excavation, uncovering a gilded menu from the hotel's restaurant, featuring decadent dishes of the era—lobster thermidor, prime rib with Yorkshire pudding, and an alarming number of aspic-based creations.

A leather-bound guest book, its pages filled with flourished signatures, spoke of travelers passing through, some leaving behind poetic musings or hurried scribbles of gratitude.

Playbills advertised grand performances: jazz quartets, traveling theater troupes, even a magician promising illusions beyond imagination!

Then, nestled carefully between the documents, was something unexpected—a delicate porcelain figurine of the Springs Hotel itself. The craftsmanship was exquisite, the tiny details capturing every balcony, every window, every Art Deco flourish.

Sadie let out a low whistle. "Someone loved this place enough to immortalize it."

Beneath it all, tucked in one final cloth-wrapped bundle, we found something even older. "This must be from the original time capsule," I murmured, unwrapping it with care.

The first thing we pulled free was a silk ribbon, now faded but still elegant, the gold lettering barely legible: *Grand Opening—The Springs Hotel, 1920.*

Beneath it, stiff-backed invitations, their Art Deco borders still gleaming faintly, promised a night of "unparalleled luxury and entertainment."

The opening gala had been a grand affair, drawing the town's elite for a night of celebration and spectacle. A leather-bound program detailed the evening's itinerary—cocktail hour in the lounge, a lavish dinner dance in the ballroom, a midnight toast under the chandeliers. The vision Colette's father had for the hotel was clear. It was never just meant to be a place to stay—it was meant to be an experience.

Newspaper clippings hailed the Springs Hotel as a marvel of modern hospitality, praising its elegant architecture and "exquisite amenities."

But it was the last item that stopped us cold.

Nestled at the bottom of the capsule was a small, crayon-colored drawing. It was childlike but lovingly detailed, the hotel's sweeping arches and grand entrance sketched with careful, uneven strokes. At the bottom, written in blocky, earnest letters, was a signature: *Colette, Age 8.*

My breath caught. "She'd loved this place her entire life."

Sadie traced the edges of the drawing reverently. "She wasn't just the owner. She was its legacy."

The weight of that realization settled over us, pressing like a heavy but welcome burden. We were holding pieces of a life that had shaped this town, and for the first time, Colette felt more than just a mystery to be solved. She felt real.

We repacked the time capsule with the care of archivists handling sacred texts, making notes as we went.

"I'll catalog everything," Sadie promised, her historian's instincts kicking in. "Maybe the hotel can put these on display. Or the university."

I hesitated. "Won't people wonder where we found it?"

Sadie's laughter was light and easy. "I'll tell them the truth—we ran across it on an old and dusty shelf."

Chapter 40

Disappearance Day

THAT NIGHT, I TOSSED and turned, too excited about our discovery to sleep.

Moonlight filtered through the curtains, casting long, silvered shadows across my room. Twila perched on my nighstand, staring at me, her eyes glowing softly, shifting between twilight hues. The colors pulsed in a slow, hypnotic rhythm—violet, sapphire, emerald—like a silent message I couldn't quite decipher.

"What is it, Twila?" I whispered.

Her faint meow shattered the stillness.

And then I knew. It wasn't just a sound. It was a summons.

I sat upright, my pulse already racing before my mind had fully caught up. I had to go back, to the day Colette disappeared.

I didn't question how I knew. I just knew. It wasn't impulse; it was something deeper. Something ancient. The truth wasn't waiting to be uncovered—it was calling me.

Every warning Eleanor and Grandma had ever given me rang in my ears, but their voices felt distant now, like echoes in a tunnel. The past was reaching out. I had to go.

A reckless certainty settled over me as I slid out of bed, my fingers trembling as I reached for my clothes.

I knew my decision stood in direct defiance of Eleanor and Grandma's dire warnings about the fragility of time. They had made it clear: tampering with the timeline could lead to devastating consequences. Yet, as I looked into Twila's otherworldly eyes, a resolve settled within me. I owed it to Colette—to her memory—to uncover the truth. If I could witness the events firsthand, maybe I could understand what had happened.

I'll just observe, I told myself. *No touching. No talking. I won't interfere.*

I reasoned with my conscience, whispering in the darkness. *I'll be a shadow. A ghost among ghosts. I won't touch anything. I won't speak to anyone. Just in and out.* The words felt hollow, but the justification gave me courage.

I slipped out of bed and tiptoed through the house, the boards beneath my feet groaning softly in protest. Twila leapt down, her spectral form gliding ahead of me, guiding the way. When I reached the shop, it was as if the storeroom beckoned me. The portal pulsed faintly, like a heartbeat in the quiet. I retrieved the 1940s dress I'd worn before, its fabric soft in my hands, and prepared myself for what felt like an inevitable journey.

I checked the logbook, reconciling the dates with Colette's disappearance. Then, with a deep breath, I stepped through the shimmering portal. Colors swirled around me, and time bent and twisted until, in an instant, I was no longer in the present.

The world of 1945 unfolded around me, vivid and alive. The streets of Enchanted Springs buzzed with energy, and the Springs Hotel stood as a beacon of activity. My heart pounded as I navigated the crowd, slipping into the building unnoticed.

Inside, the lobby hummed with the sounds of 1940s elegance: the distant clink of glasses, the murmur of conversations, and the faint strains of a jazz piano drifting from the lounge. My chest tightened as I moved through the opulent space, every detail a stark reminder of the living, breathing past.

I spotted Natasha near the stairwell to the basement. Her movements were hurried, almost frantic. She glanced over her shoulder, her expression a mixture of paranoia and determination.

My pulse raced as I hesitated, then followed her down the narrow stairs. The air grew cooler with each step, the walls closing in as I descended into the dimly lit space.

The air grew colder as I descended. Stone walls closed in, the damp scent of mildew, old wood, and something vaguely metallic. A single dim bulb flickered overhead, casting warped, shifting shadows that slithered across the walls.

The ceiling was low, crisscrossed with exposed beams and tangled pipes that dripped occasionally, adding to the oppressive atmosphere. The floor was uneven, a mix of cracked concrete and dirt that muffled my footsteps but sent faint echoes into the shadowed corners.

Natasha was at the far end of the room, struggling to drag an old steamer trunk across the floor. Her breath came in sharp, ragged bursts, her cheeks flushed with exertion. The trunk's brass fittings glinted faintly in the dim light, and the scrape of its worn edges against the floor sent a shiver up my spine. Her hands, pale and trembling, gripped the trunk as though it held the weight of the world—or a secret too heavy to bear.

The faint creak of a pipe above us made her head snap up, her expression hardening into one of suspicion. Her eyes narrowed, flashing with a dangerous light. "What are you doing here?" she snapped, her voice cutting through the silence like a blade.

"I lost my cat," I stammered. "I thought she might have come down here."

Her lips curled into a sneer, and she stepped toward me, her presence menacing. "Nice try," she hissed. "You're not from around here. What are you really looking for?"

My throat tightened. "What's in the trunk?"

Her face twisted with rage. "That's none of your business. Get out. Now."

I backed toward the stairs, but before I could retreat, Natasha lunged, picking up a hammer that had been lying on the floor. Her grip was white-knuckled, her knuckles pale against the dark, worn handle. The hammer's head gleamed dully in the dim light, a brutal contrast to the soft glow of the bulb overhead.

"You shouldn't have come here," she growled, her voice low and venomous, the kind of tone that raised every hair on the back of my neck.

I swallowed hard. "What's in the trunk, Natasha?"

Her darkened gaze burned through me. "Nothing that concerns you." She stepped toward me.

I stepped back.

Natasha tilted her head. Too far. Too unnatural. Then, slowly—too slowly—she smiled, a wicked, knowing grin.

I ducked just in time as she swung the hammer, the air whistling with its deadly arc. The hammer in her grip whistled past my face, missing by inches. The force of the miss sent her staggering forward, her breath coming in sharp, furious bursts.

"You're insane!" I shouted, my heart pounding like a war drum.

"Perhaps." Her eyes burned with a dangerous intensity, her wild movements throwing erratic shadows onto the walls. She advanced, her steps deliberate and predatory.

Adrenaline surged through me as I scrambled backward, my foot catching on a rusted metal bucket that clattered loudly. Natasha's grip tightened as she swung again, the hammer striking a support beam with a sickening thud. Dust rained down from the ceiling, and the faint groan of the structure added to the growing tension. The sound seemed to echo my heartbeat, a frantic rhythm in the oppressive stillness.

"Stay back!" I yelled, grabbing the nearest object—a long, rusted pipe. I held it out like a makeshift shield. My arms trembled under the weight, but I refused to let her see my fear.

With a burst of courage, I lunged, knocking the hammer from her grasp. It clattered to the floor, the sound echoing like a gunshot in the confined space. For a moment, the room was filled with nothing but the sound of our heavy breaths, each one a testament to the chaos of the moment.

Then, a blur of motion caught my eye. Twila. She leapt through the air, landing on Natasha's head with claws extended, her spectral form shimmering with a faint, otherworldly light.

Natasha shrieked, clawing at the cat as Twila scratched at her face, her tiny body a whirlwind of defiance. The faint glow from Twila's form cast eerie shadows on the walls, amplifying the surreal nature of the scene.

"Twila, come on!" I shouted, bolting up the stairs, taking them two at a time. Natasha's enraged screams echoed behind me as I sprinted up the narrow staircase, my heart pounding in rhythm with the frantic slap of my footsteps.

As I raced through the lobby, I barely spared a glance at the startled faces of a couple of guests lingering near the front desk. I bolted through the grand entrance and onto the darkened streets of Enchanted Springs.

The night air hit me like a slap as I bolted onto Main Street.

Behind me, Natasha's voice rang out, filled with fury. "You can't run from me!"

I sprinted down Main Street, the shadows of the old buildings stretching long and distorted under the flickering glow of the streetlamps. A bewildered man in a fedora stepped aside as I dashed past, his confused gaze following me. A woman walking her dog froze, clutching her pet close as Natasha barreled after me, her face twisted with rage.

The antique shop was in sight, its familiar facade a beacon of safety. My breath burned in my chest as I reached the door, fumbling with the key. Natasha's footsteps grew louder, her curses echoing in the empty street.

Finally, the lock turned, and I flung the door open, slipping inside and slamming it shut just as Natasha reached the stoop. Her fists pounded against the glass, her face contorted with frustration. "You can't hide forever!" she spat, her voice muffled but still venomous.

I backed away, my chest heaving, as Twila curled around my ankles, her spectral form glowing faintly in the dim light of the shop. Natasha's figure lingered outside for a moment longer, her furious eyes meeting mine through the glass. Then, with a final snarl, she turned and disappeared into the shadows.

The portal shimmered faintly in the storeroom, its light a comforting glow. I collapsed onto the floor, gasping for breath. My heart thundered in my chest. Twila padded over, her ethereal form curling up beside me as if nothing had happened.

The past wasn't just haunting me.

It was hunting me.

Chapter 41

The Scene of the Crime

As I stumbled out of the storage room, the front door burst open. Jack Edgewood came in, eyes narrowed, surveying the shop.

"Marley, are you all right? The shop's silent alarms went off at the station."

My hands trembled slightly, a physical echo of the adrenaline still coursing through me, and my breathing was heavy and ragged, as if I'd run three miles instead of three blocks. I really needed to start working out.

He stepped closer as he took in my disheveled appearance. Before I could respond, he was by my side, his hand steadying me with a touch that carried both reassurance and unspoken questions. His gaze swept over me, searching for any sign of injury or distress.

He was too close. Distractingly close. The scent of clean cedarwood and something faintly smoky—whiskey? leather?—clung to him. His chiseled jaw tensed as his gaze swept over me, taking in every detail.

I swallowed hard. "I'm okay, Jack," I managed, though my voice was still shaky. "But I think I know what happened to Colette."

His expression darkened, the lines of his face sharpening. "Tell me."

I took a deep breath, the night's terror still clinging to my skin like static electricity. "I might have broken a few time-travel rules, but I'm pretty sure Natasha killed her and hid her body in the hotel basement."

Jack's gaze sharpened. His grip on my arms tightened just slightly before he let go. "A trunk?"

I nodded. ""It was big enough for a body," I said, my voice trembling slightly. "When I spotted her trying to drag it across the basement floor, she attacked me."

His jaw clenched, the muscle ticking just beneath the shadow of stubble on his cheek. "Do you think it's still there?"

I hesitated, searching for the right words. "I'm not sure, but the basement back then felt different, somehow. And there was something about that trunk, Jack. It was heavy, and Natasha was completely unhinged."

For a moment, Jack said nothing, his gaze locked onto mine with an intensity that made my breath catch. Then, with a nod, he turned on his heel. "Let's go."

We hurried down the street to the Springs Hotel, our footsteps in sync. Jack's broad frame was tense with focus, his presence an unshakable force beside me.

I was still dressed in my 1940s costume, which raised some eyebrows—but not as many as Jack when he flashed his badge at the front desk clerk, his tone authoritative but calm. "We'll need access to the basement."

A moment later, we stood at the top of the basement stairwell, the door creaking open to reveal the dim, shadowy descent.

Jack pulled out a heavy-duty flashlight and flicked it on, the bright beam slicing through the darkness.

"This is where I saw Natasha with the trunk," I said as we stepped cautiously into the cool, damp air of the basement.

The space was as eerie as I remembered, the weak light from bare bulbs casting long, distorted shadows across the rough-hewn stone walls. The air was heavy with the scent of mildew and something faintly metallic, and the faint dripping of water echoed like a distant heartbeat.

Jack scanned the room, his flashlight sweeping over the clutter of forgotten equipment and debris. "Show me exactly where she was," he instructed, his voice steady.

I pointed toward a corner of the basement where the air seemed heavier, the darkness more oppressive. "She was over there, dragging the trunk. But now I realize what was so different. That wall wasn't here in 1945. Look at the bricks—they don't match."

Jack frowned, stepping closer to inspect the uneven brickwork. He reached out, running his hand over the surface. "You're right. This was probably added decades after the hotel was built."

I moved forward, compelled by a mix of intuition and determination. "I think it's a false wall," I said, tapping on the bricks. The hollow sound that echoed back sent a chill down my spine.

"Marley, don't," Jack warned, his tone sharp. "If there's evidence behind this wall, we need to follow the law."

I shot him a defiant look. "Jack, Colette's murder happened decades ago. Natasha's not alive anymore, and this isn't an active crime scene. Evidence laws don't apply here."

He hesitated, his jaw clenching. "You're not wrong, but..."

"In for a penny, in for a pound," I muttered. I thumped at the wall. The mortar crumbled under my touch, and a few bricks tumbled inward, revealing a narrow, shadowed cavity. Jack sighed, his frustration evident, but he didn't stop me as I pulled away more bricks, widening the opening.

Inside the cavity, nestled in the shadows, was an old steamer trunk. Its leather surface was cracked and worn, the brass fittings tarnished but still gleaming faintly in the dim light. My breath caught as I reached for the lid.

Jack's hand shot out, gripping my wrist gently but firmly. "Marley, are you sure about this?"

I nodded, my resolve unwavering. "If Colette's in there, we need to know."

He released my wrist, stepping back but keeping the flashlight trained on the trunk. I gripped the edges of the lid, my fingers trembling as I lifted it. The hinges groaned in protest, the sound echoing in the stillness.

Inside, the skeletal remains of a woman lay tucked in the faded remnants of a dress, the fabric rotted and brittle. Colette. Even after decades, I could still see a faint shimmer of pearls at her throat.

Jack exhaled sharply, his flashlight illuminating the delicate curve of the skull. "If she was poisoned, there might still be traces in her bones," he murmured. He hesitated, then pointed to a fracture that split the skull. "But if I had to guess, I'd say this was the cause of death."

As I processed the scene, a sharp pang of realization struck me. "My charm bracelet," I said, holding up my bare wrist. "It's gone."

Chapter 42

Together at Last

BEFORE JACK COULD RESPOND, a soft, golden glow began to spread through the basement, illuminating the crumbling brick walls with a warmth that felt impossibly out of place in such a forgotten, timeworn space. The shadows that had once clung to the corners recoiled, retreating as if banished by the light's quiet power.

The very air around us felt charged—not with fear, but with something softer, something sacred. The scent of orange blossoms—delicate and fleeting—drifted through the room, and the temperature rose just enough to chase away the lingering chill.

Then, she appeared.

Colette.

Her spirit materialized before us, her form luminous, shimmering with the soft glow of dawn's first light. Unlike the flickering, fragmented images I had seen before—ghostly echoes half-lost to time—this Colette was whole, radiant. She was finally free.

I stilled, my breath catching in my throat.

Her hair, once pinned in meticulous waves, now cascaded freely over her shoulders, catching the light as though spun from fire and silk. The pearl earrings she had worn in life still adorned her ears, gleaming softly, and her familiar cream-colored suit had taken on a dreamlike shimmer, its fabric moving with a weightless grace.

Her gaze, filled with warmth and something achingly eternal, met mine.

I felt her gratitude before she spoke it.

Slowly, she extended her hand, and resting in her palm was my bracelet.

The delicate silver charms glowed softly, each one pulsing faintly as if infused with some lingering magic. When her fingers brushed mine, a warmth passed through me—not heat, not static, but something deeper. A connection. A pulse of understanding older than time itself.

Tears burned behind my eyes as I accepted the bracelet, its weight heavier now, imbued with something more than just metal and memory.

"Thank you," Colette whispered, her voice a melody that resonated in the very marrow of my bones. "You freed me from the prison that held me bound to this world. You brought the truth to light."

Jack and I stood frozen, watching as she turned toward the glow that had begun to expand behind her, its golden radiance stretching outward, beckoning.

And then—from the light—a figure emerged.

Tall, dark-haired, with the same devastating smile that had charmed the entire hotel, Ricardo Rios stepped forward.

But this was not the Ricardo I had seen in life—not the calculated charmer at the bar, nor the man struggling beneath the weight of unspoken tensions.

This Ricardo was whole, unburdened, his presence radiant in a way that no living soul could ever be. His dark eyes were shining with love, and when he stretched his arms wide, it was not with the careless ease of a flirt, but with the undeniable certainty of a man who had waited lifetimes.

Colette gasped.

For a moment, she simply stood, her form trembling as if she hardly dared believe.

Then—she ran.

Her feet didn't quite touch the ground, but she moved with the force of a woman who had spent decades aching for this moment.

Ricardo caught her, lifting her into his arms, and their reunion radiated a joy that transcended everything—time, loss, even death.

Jack let out a slow exhale beside me, and when I glanced at him, his expression was unreadable.

But something in his stormy blue eyes had softened. I think I saw a flicker of recognition and understanding.

I turned back as the light around Colette and Ricardo intensified, wrapping them in its golden embrace. The basement—a place of sorrow, of darkness—now pulsed with warmth. The very walls seemed to breathe, releasing the centuries-old grief that had clung to them.

The last thing I saw before the light consumed them completely was the way Ricardo pressed his forehead against Colette's, whispering something only she could hear.

Then they were gone.

The glow dissipated, fading like the last embers of a candle. The oppressive weight of the room lifted, leaving behind a quiet so profound it felt sacred.

Jack and I stood in the aftermath, the echoes of their departure still humming in the air.

I glanced down at the bracelet in my palm, the metal warm as though still carrying the imprint of Colette's touch.

The Springs Hotel had finally released its secrets—and Colette and Ricardo had finally found their way home.

Chapter 43

Love Conquers All

THERE WAS A DEEP sigh behind us. I turned just in time to see Irwin's ghost emerge from the shadows, his form shimmering softly, like a memory struggling to stay whole. He had finally crept down from the attic, drawn here by the same pull of unfinished stories and long-buried truths.

His expression was a storm of emotions—sorrow, relief, longing.

His gaze flickered to the place where Colette and Ricardo had stood moments ago, where the golden light had swallowed them whole, carrying them to whatever lay beyond. His spectral chest rose and fell in a slow, wistful breath, though it was only a habit of his former life.

"I'm glad," he murmured, his voice weighted with years of quiet suffering. "If anyone deserved a happy ending, it was Colette."

Jack and I exchanged a glance, but before we could speak, a cold wind swept through the basement.

The air grew heavier, thicker, crackling with unrest.

And then, like a spectral zombie, Natasha crawled out through the opening in the wall, stumbling and staggering over the fallen bricks.

Her form wasn't like Colette's. Where Colette had radiated warmth, Natasha's spirit rippled with torment, her shape flickering, unstable—as if she were barely holding herself together. Her eyes were haunted and hollow, and her hands clutched at her chest, her spectral fingers twisting in anguish.

Her lips trembled as she opened her mouth. "I'm so sorry," she whispered, her voice raw, as though she had spent decades choking on those words.

"I don't know what I was thinking. I was wrong—so wrong—to try to steal another woman's husband. I was even more deluded to think that I could get by with murder. And it all backfired so horribly."

Her form shuddered, a convulsion of pain rippling through her ghostly body.

"You can't imagine what it's been like—condemned to this godforsaken cellar, trapped with the body of the woman I killed. It's been hell on earth. But the worst part is the fact that I deserve it."

Her voice cracked, and she bowed her head, as if crushed beneath the weight of her own confession.

The words hung in the air, thick as smoke, and for the first time, I saw Natasha not as a murderer, not as a villain—but as a woman who had shattered her own soul.

Irwin stepped forward. His glow, once faint, now pulsed with something steadier. And his voice, when he spoke, was so gentle, so filled with aching, buried love, that it made my breath hitch.

"I could have stopped you," he said softly.

Natasha's head snapped up, her tear-streaked face frozen in shock.

Irwin's gaze never wavered. "I knew you were tortured, both in life and in death. I should have spoken up. I should have told you... I loved you."

Natasha made a sound—half gasp, half sob.

She swayed, as if his words had physically hit her.

"You... what?" she whispered. Her hands, still trembling, lowered from her chest, as if letting go of something invisible.

Irwin smiled, small and sad, the kind of smile that held a lifetime of regret.

"I loved you, Natasha," he repeated, the words steady, unshakable. "The whole time we worked together, I watched you from across the lobby, pining for you, wishing I had the courage to tell you how I felt."

Her mouth opened and closed a few times, her translucent form trembling as if trying to process his words. Tears shimmered in her spectral eyes, and she took a tentative step toward him. "Oh, Irwin. How I wish I'd known. Everything could have been different."

And then—so softly I almost didn't hear it—she laughed.

A small, broken sound.

"What a fool I was," she murmured. "All that time, chasing after a man who never really saw me, while the one who truly did... stood right in front of me."

My throat ached with emotion. Now I was crying. Probably ugly crying. I could even feel my nose starting to run.

I felt the warmth of Jack's hand on my shoulder.

When I looked at him, his stormy blue eyes were shadowed with something deep—something distant. His jaw was tight, his lips pressed together as if he were holding back words he wasn't ready to say.

Irwin and Natasha still stood, facing each other.

Natasha took a hesitant step forward.

"Irwin, I'm so sorry," she said, her voice breaking. "For everything. If only I had seen what was right in front of me, maybe none of this would have happened."

Irwin reached out, his hand hovering just shy of touching hers. "Natasha, if it's any consolation, I forgive you. And I hope you can find it in yourself to forgive me, too."

For a moment, they simply looked at each other, two souls intertwined by fate and tragedy, each seeking solace in the other's forgiveness. Then, as if guided by an unseen force, they stepped closer, their forms beginning to shimmer with a soft, ethereal light.

Jack leaned in slightly, his voice barely audible as he whispered, "Look." His hand lingered on my shoulder, his warmth steadying me against the overwhelming emotions of the moment.

The light around Natasha and Irwin grew brighter, casting their shadows against the storied walls of the cellar. There was no fanfare, no trumpets or angel wings—just a gentle radiance that seemed to embrace them, wrapping them in warmth and peace. The light seemed to ripple outward, brushing against Jack and me with a faint warmth that left goosebumps in its wake.

As we watched, the light swirled, a dance of particles and energy that enveloped Natasha and Irwin, lifting them from the earthly confines of guilt and remorse. Their faces, once marred by the anguish of their actions, softened, revealing a hint of the joy and relief that comes with absolution.

Natasha turned to Irwin, her hand finally reaching for his. When their fingers intertwined, the light around them surged, as if their connection had completed the circuit. A soft smile graced her lips, and she whispered, "Thank you."

"And thank you," Irwin replied, his voice steady, though his eyes shone with unshed tears. "For giving me the courage to say what I've felt all along."

Their forms grew brighter, almost too dazzling to look at, and with a soft sigh that seemed to echo through the cellar, they were gone. The light faded, leaving behind an empty space where two tortured souls had once stood, a last testament to their journey from darkness to redemption.

In the silence that followed, I wiped away my tears, a sense of closure settling in my heart. Colette's story, and those intertwined with hers, had found their ending—not in the pages of a history book, but in the cosmic forgiveness that offered them a second chance at eternal happiness.

Jack and I stood there for a moment longer, the echoes of their departure lingering in the air like a fading melody. He let out a long breath, his hand still resting on my shoulder. When I glanced up at him, I saw something in his eyes—a mixture of awe, tenderness, and something unspoken that made my heart skip a beat.

"Marley," he said softly, his voice low and filled with an emotion I couldn't quite name. "Witnessing that makes you realize what's really important, doesn't it?"

I nodded, unable to trust my voice. The way he looked at me, the way his hand lingered just a moment longer than necessary—it was as if the boundaries we'd maintained were beginning to blur, softened by the light of redemption we'd just witnessed.

"Come on," Jack finally said, his tone gentle but steady. "Let's get out of here. We've got a lot to process."

As we climbed the stairs, leaving the basement behind, the air felt lighter, as if the weight of the past had finally lifted. But even as we stepped into the cool night, the warmth of Jack's presence beside me lingered, a quiet reminder that some stories were just beginning.

Chapter 44

The Greek

BACK AT THE ENCHANTED Oven, I sat with Grandma Clara and Eleanor, a cup of coffee warming my hands.

The events of the past few days felt surreal, as though I had slipped between the pages of a novel and lived a dozen lifetimes in the span of a weekend—but the truth had been uncovered.

In front of me, my coffee sat untouched, its steam curling in lazy wisps as I turned my charm bracelet over in my fingers. The tiny silver hourglass charm glinted softly under the overhead lights, its meaning far heavier than its delicate size.

Across from me, Gram and Eleanor sipped their coffee with the kind of slow, deliberate patience that told me they were waiting for me to spill everything.

I took a deep breath. "I found Colette."

Gram set her coffee cup down so abruptly that it sloshed over the rim, a few stray drops splattering onto the table.

"You what?"

Eleanor turned toward my grandmother and repeated my words, loudly, in her ear. "She says she found Colette, dear."

Gram swatted her away impatiently. "I heard her just fine, Eleanor. I just couldn't believe what I heard."

Eleanor raised her eyebrows and reached for a bear claw. "What's so hard to understand? She found Colette!" Then she paused, pastry in mid-air, and turned back toward me, her expression more serious.

They listened quietly as I recounted every detail—from stepping through the portal to my final, heart-pounding sprint away from Natasha's ghost. Their faces shifted with every twist of the tale, from shock to concern to absolute exasperation.

When I described how Colette's ghost had handed me my charm bracelet—an act that defied the very laws of magic and time—Eleanor's bear claw slipped from her fingers, forgotten.

Gram, however, was laser-focused on something else entirely. She folded her arms, her mouth set in a thin line. "So let me get this straight."

I braced myself for a scolding, feeling like I was ten again..

"You climbed out of bed in the middle of the night."

Uh-oh.

"Traveled back in time."

Well, yeah.

"By yourself."

That could have been in error in judgment.

"Without permission, and without telling anyone?"

I nodded, shrinking under the weight of her stare. Now that I heard it out loud, it sounded much, much worse.

Eleanor and Gram exchanged a glance. One of those long, silent, we-are-too-old-for-this kind of glances.

Then Gram exhaled sharply, rubbing her temples as if she had a time-travel-induced headache. "Marley, your trip wasn't just ill-advised—it was reckless. You weren't just interfering with the timeline. You were courting danger on a level you might not fully appreciate."

Eleanor nodded in agreement. "You put yourself in grave peril, my dear."

The gravity of my actions struck me as I saw their expressions. I had disrupted the timeline. I could have torn the fabric of space and time. Worse, I could have been killed.

Gram's expression softened as she reached across the table, taking my hand in hers. "But then again, you did something remarkable. You brought closure to a story that's haunted this town for decades. You've done a great service to Colette's memory."

Eleanor sighed, shaking her head as she picked up her forgotten bear claw. "You've shown remarkable courage, Marley. But with great power comes great responsibility."

I blinked. "Did you just quote Spider Man at me?"

Eleanor took a thoughtful bite of pastry. "Perhaps. The kid had a point."

The bell over the door chimed, interrupting the moment. We all turned toward the sound, and there, framed in the doorway, stood a dark, bearded figure.

The shift in the air was immediate.

I recognized him instantly. My breath caught in my throat as the memory surfaced: I had seen him at the hotel bar in 1945. And today, he wore the same unassuming attire—a simple, well-tailored dark jacket, a crisp white shirt, and plain black trousers. It was the perfect look for a time traveler, understated and unremarkable in any era.

His presence, however, was anything but subtle. An undeniable aura of knowledge and authority surrounded him.

As he stepped toward us, the air seemed to thrum with an unspoken power. The lights dimmed, and the usual sounds of the day faded into a deafening silence. I glanced up at the clock on the wall and noticed it had stopped ticking.

Eleanor and Gram stood simultaneously, their postures rigid, a clear sign of the gravity of the moment.

My grandmother spoke first. "Is there a problem?"

His gaze swept the room, landing on me with an intensity that felt almost tangible. "There is," he confirmed, his voice calm but carrying an undeniable weight. "We've been observing Marley's training."

I swallowed hard.

"It hasn't escaped our notice that in less than a week of her initiation, Marley has taken several unconventional moves, completely unsupervised."

My grandmother opened her mouth to speak, but the man raised his hand to silence her.

"Luckily, the damage was minimal."

"What damage?" I asked. "Is it something I can fix?"

He paused, tilting his head slightly as if contemplating my question.

"Thankfully, the damage was minimal. "Take the name of the Opal Hush wine bar, for instance."

I blinked. "What about it?"

He folded his arms, his expression unreadable. "Before your interference with the timeline, the establishment was set to be known as... the Citrus Spritzer Lounge."

I gaped at him. Gram slapped a hand to her forehead. Eleanor snorted into her coffee.

I blinked, startled, before blurting out, "Well, Opal Hush is definitely an upgrade."

For the first time, something flickered in the man's eyes. A glint of something dangerously close to amusement.

"Be that as it may," he said, "you must understand that even seemingly minor changes can ripple outward in unexpected ways."

I swallowed hard, the gravity of his words sinking in. A vivid memory flashed through my mind, casting my recent journeys in a stark, new light. I remembered standing at the bar, turning toward Natasha with a look of empathy as Ricardo gazed lovingly at Colette. In that moment, filled with the tense possibility of connection, what if Natasha had seen me as a confidante? What if she had looked to me as someone to unburden her soul to?

The thought of Natasha, driven by desperation or a moment of vulnerability, reaching out for guidance, advice, or even a plea for help, now seemed like a narrow escape. I couldn't have said no—but I could easily have altered the course of history. The weight of "what if" settled heavily on my shoulders.

The risks I had taken, driven by a desire to uncover the truth and seek justice, suddenly felt recklessly naïve.

He let my silence speak for itself. Then he turned to Eleanor and Gram.

"Ensure a closer eye is kept on Marley." His voice was final. "The consequences of further unauthorized interventions in the timeline could be dire, not just for Marley, but for the fabric of reality itself."

Gram placed a reassuring hand on my shoulder, a silent pledge of their support and guidance. "We will take your warning to heart," she said, her voice firm. "Marley's talents are a gift, but we recognize the need for restraint and guidance."

"In that case, I'll bid you farewell."

With that, he turned and left, as quietly as he had arrived. The bell chimed, and the room snapped back to normal.

I let out a breath I hadn't realized I'd been holding.

His warning hung in the air, a stark reminder of the balance between curiosity and caution, between the desire to act and the need to understand the potential repercussions of those actions.

Eleanor and Grandma Clara sat back down, their expressions serious but not unkind.

I looked from one to the other. "Who was that man?"

"That, my dear, was someone you probably wouldn't have met for many years, if you had followed our instructions. His name is Alex Mercer, and he's a member of the Higher Council of Guardians, which oversees our work here in Enchanted Springs."

"But I recognized him. He was at the bar in Colette's hotel."

Gram raised her eyebrows. "Was he? Interesting."

"I wonder if he's the one they called 'The Greek.'"

Eleanor shrugged. "Perhaps. He does have that look."

Gram turned toward me. "Maybe someday we can ask him—but not too soon, Marley. Not too soon."

Chapter 45

Sadie's Big Reveal

THE ENCHANTED ANTIQUE SHOP was quiet that morning, the usual hum of curious customers replaced by a serene stillness. Grandma Clara, Eleanor, and I sat around the small table near the shop's front window, the scent of freshly brewed coffee mingling with the faint aroma of antique wood and aged paper.

I was flipping through the latest edition of the Enchanted Springs Weekly when my eyes landed on the headline that made me sit up straighter: "Professor's Research Cracks Decades-Old Mystery: Colette Rios Found at Last." A photograph of Sadie accompanied the article, her confident smile radiating triumph.

Gram leaned over, her curiosity piqued. "What's that, dear?"

I turned the paper toward her, pointing to the article. "Sadie found a way to explain everything. According to this, her research into the Springs Hotel led to the discovery of Colette's remains."

"Clever," Eleanor said, sipping her tea. "It's a good cover."

Just then, the doorbell jingled, and in walked Sadie herself, wearing an expression that could only be described as victorious.

"Please tell me you've read the paper."

"We were just admiring your handiwork," I said, holding up the front page. "Quite the headline."

Sadie perched on a stool, brushing an imaginary speck of dust off her sleeve. "Well, I figured if we were going to explain how Colette's body was found, we might as well do it in style."

"And take all the credit," I teased, though I couldn't help but smile.

"Credit where it's due," she shot back with a wink. "The article explains that I was researching the hotel's history for an upcoming lecture—which, by the way, I've been invited to present to the Sunshine State Heritage Association next month. While combing through old property records, I 'discovered' a reference to a sealed-off area in the basement."

Gram nodded approvingly. "Well done. It ties everything up nicely."

"Exactly. So I 'notified' Jack and the historical society, and he investigated." Sadie's tone turned somber. "The article highlights Colette's story—her contributions to the town and the tragedy of her disappearance—without delving into the more paranormal aspects."

I laughed, feeling a weight lift from my shoulders. "You're a genius, Sadie."

"Don't I know it? But seriously, Marley, you and Jack did the hard part. I just made sure the world understood the discovery in a way they could accept."

Eleanor raised her cup. "To Colette Rios. May her story finally rest in peace."

We clinked our cups together, a quiet toast in the morning light. For the first time in days, I felt a sense of closure—not just for Colette, but for myself. Sadie's quick thinking had given us all a way to honor the past without endangering the future.

As we sipped our coffee, the shop door opened once more, and Violet floated in, wearing a feathered hat and a smile that could charm the devil himself. "What did I miss?"

Gram handed her the paper, a twinkle in her eye. "Just a bit of history being made, Violet. Just a bit of history."

Chapter 46

Founders Festival

S UDDENLY, IT WAS FRIDAY. The week had flown by in a whirlwind of emotions and revelations. Between the time travels and the historic discoveries we'd made, I felt as though I'd lived several lifetimes in just a few days.

I laughed to myself. I had experienced decades of tumult in the blink of an eye. It made me wonder how Eleanor and Grandma Clara coped, having spent years immersed in this blend of past and present, their lives a tapestry woven from the threads of countless eras.

But now, the Founders Festival was finally here. After a night of deep, restorative sleep—the kind that seemed to wash away the residue of decades—I woke up feeling refreshed and eager for the day ahead.

I was ready for some fun.

People had lined up along the parade route hours before it was scheduled to start. They brought lawn chairs and camping chairs, staking their claims to Main Street's prime sidewalk real estate. Many had coolers with soft drinks and snacks, and every shop and storefront that sold food was busy with lines out the door.

Some were even in costume, dressed like old pioneers. Women wore long dresses and bonnets. Men wore flannel shirts and denim overalls. Enchanted Springs had been settled originally by Civil War veterans, mostly from the North, but reenactors sported costumes from both sides, and saluted each other accordingly.

Grandma and Kate kept the bakery open until the parade was scheduled to start, then flipped the closed sign and hurried outside, where Eleanor and I had saved them a spot.

"Here they come!" Grandma's voice cut through the growing buzz of the crowd as the parade came down the street, led by a brigade of fire trucks and police cars, their sirens a celebratory wail. Beside her, Eleanor and I found ourselves amidst a crowd that was unlike any I had seen before—a mix of the living and the dead, each as excited as the other.

The parade was a vibrant display of Enchanted Springs' rich history. Actors in period costumes stood proudly on floats, depicting figures from the town's past with a zeal that seemed to collapse the years between us. I smiled when I realized I could see their spectral counterparts standing next to them, glowing with happiness. They were more than simply echoes of the past; they were very much a part of our present celebration.

My gaze followed a float dedicated to Henry Addison, the bearded "baking soda king" who had invested his fortune into the land on which we stood. I couldn't help noting both the actor's flamboyant portrayal and the gentle, approving nod from Henry's spirit beside him.

Sarah Addison, his wife and the town's first postmaster—or postmistress, as she'd likely prefer—was there too. She wore a long dark skirt, a ruffled blouse with a high collar, and a fetching 1880s hair style, sleekly parted down the middle, pulled into a bun, and offset with perfectly waved bangs. I wondered for a minute if I could do the same with my thick, wavy hair.

Eleanor's voice brought me back to the moment. "It's remarkable, isn't it? The way the past and present meld here. It makes history feel alive." Her eyes briefly met mine before turning back to the parade.

The Addisons were followed in short order by Theodore and Elizabeth Stevens, founders of the Philadelphia hat-making dynasty. The two regal figures had spent winters in Enchanted Springs, in a sprawling Victorian mansion.

The actors who portrayed them were riding in an open carriage pulled by a team of horses, with a driver in front. It's a good thing the carriage had two rows of seats, because the ghosts of the real, live Stevens—I mean, the real, dead Stevens—were in the back seat.

The crowd was a lively tapestry woven from the threads of many eras, where the laughter and cheers of the living mingled with the softer, ethereal echoes of the dead. Children, in their timeless innocence, interacted with both the costumed actors and their ghostly complements, their delight a beautiful reminder of the magic that coursed through Enchanted Springs.

As the Magnolia University float passed us, I stood and cheered for Sadie. At my suggestion, she had hastily recruited members of the school's drama club, who were more than happy to dress in Shakespearean costumes and recite lines of Romeo and Juliet to the crowd.

In almost every subsequent float and parade entry, I noticed participants who probably weren't obvious to most onlookers. Their costumes were perfectly on point, and they all seemed to have the same radiant glow. They could hop on and hop off the parade floats and cars with no concern: one minute they'd be in the back seat of a convertible, or riding on the flatbed of a truck, and the next they'd be in the crowd on the sidewalk, gently reaching out to embrace a spectator. Most of their interaction went unacknowledged—except by children, who squealed with delight and waved back, or even reached out to touch them as they drew near.

Watching the parade with Grandma Clara and Eleanor, I felt a deep connection to Enchanted Springs and its inhabitants, past and present. The parade wasn't just a celebration; it was a living, breathing homage to those who had shaped our town—a legacy I was part of.

As the last notes of the parade faded, leaving behind a resonant silence filled with the echoes of the day, we lingered a moment longer, watching as the spectral participants faded, their presence a gentle benediction on the day's festivities.

"That was a fantastic kickoff," Grandma Clara declared, her tone rich with satisfaction. "And now, onward and upward to Courthouse Square!"

Chapter 47

The Dance

COURTHOUSE SQUARE HAD BEEN transformed into a magical fantasy land, like something out of a movie. The World's Fair Fountain was illuminated with colored lights, while all around us vendors, artists, and crafters sold art, artifacts, and souvenirs.

All around us, people walked. Singles, couples, families. There were old people with walkers, young families with strollers, couples holding hands. No one was alone.

I navigated through the crowd, soaking in the vibrant energy of Enchanted Springs. Amidst the bustle, a distinct voice caught my attention, drawing my gaze to a figure that seemed to command the space around her—Madame Endora.

Draped in colorful scarves, with an enigmatic smile playing on her lips, she beckoned me closer. "Marley, dear," she greeted, her voice rich with an accent that spoke of faraway places. "I've been watching your journey with great interest. The stars have much to say about you."

I nodded. "Grandma Clara mentioned you checked my transits."

"Yes, and there's more to discuss. You should stop by my parlor soon. You're at a crossroads, and the universe holds additional guidance and advice for you."

Over at the bandstand, a small crowd was gathering as the mayor took the stage. She tapped the standing microphone and welcomed the crowd.

"Ladies, gentlemen, neighbors and friends, the spirit of the pioneers lives in us all who choose Enchanted Springs as a place to live, work, and play." She had no idea how right she was. "It is my distinct honor as your honor to welcome each and every one of you to the Founders Festival."

She announced several honors and awards. I noticed some ghosts and spirits giggling a bit as the prize for best costume went to a woman who supposedly embodied the "pioneer spirit" of Enchanted Springs. Unfortunately, her costume was a mishmash of eras—she wore a Victorian corset over an Edwardian gown, cowboy boots, and a coonskin cap. The actual pioneers of Enchanted Springs, observing from their ethereal vantage point, found her eclectic ensemble hilariously inaccurate, a charming yet bewildering homage to their time.

Then came the announcement we'd been waiting for. "The blue ribbon for this year's best pie goes to... Clara Montgomery!" the mayor proclaimed, her voice carrying over the crowd. Cheers erupted as Grandma Clara, with a modest smile, accepted her prize.

But the mayor wasn't finished. "We have another special recognition today," she continued, turning to address the gathering more formally. "It's for someone who has dedicated her life not only to preserving the past, safeguarding our history, and highlighting our own unique Enchanted Springs heritage."

The crowd fell into an expectant hush as the mayor gestured toward our little group. "For her unwavering commitment to historic preservation through the Enchanted Antique Shop, we are proud to award Eleanor Somerville the Heritage Guardian Award."

Applause filled the air as Eleanor, visibly moved, accepted the award—a beautifully crafted bronze plaque.

The crowd cheered, and my grandmother squeezed my hand, grinning from ear to ear. "I'm so glad you came home for this, Marley. Oh, my goodness, this is so exciting!"

I had been taking photos all day, of both the living and their corporeally challenged counterparts. Everywhere I looked, both on camera and off, I saw ghosts. They blended seamlessly with the crowd, milling about, playing carnival games, greeting friends, chatting, admiring lights and decorations and costumes, even interacting with pets. They looked almost like normal people—except for the fact that they glowed. They were just a little bit lighter and brighter than living people. They didn't have auras: they were auras. They weren't spirits with bodies. They were just spirits. Most seemed to leave a faint trail of stars as they walked.

Then I spotted a spectral figure who didn't fit in with the usual crowd of Enchanted Spring's nearest and dearest departed. I leaned over and whispered in my grandmother's ear. "Is that Ponce DeLeon?"

I nodded subtly toward the explorer's ghost. He looked just like the paintings and statues that popped up at tourist traps all around the state, wherever community groups could claim a sulfur spring as the original, authentic, legendary Fountain of Youth.

"Why yes, dear, I believe it is. Oh, those Spaniards had such style."

"Are you saying that our town fountain is the Fountain of Youth?"

"Well, not youth, obviously, or I wouldn't have nearly so many laugh lines. It might be more accurate to say that the World's Fair Fountain channels a certain magic power that keeps everything lively."

Someone rang an old-fashioned dinner bell, and we all lined up for a catered barbecue. The menu was unabashedly Southern: Pulled pork sandwiches, potato salad, coleslaw, baked beans, collard greens, and gallons of sweet tea. And for dessert? Sour orange pie.

Later, as the sun set, casting a golden hue over the town, the crowd moved into the street between the Courthouse and Courthouse Square. Music filled the air, couples danced in the street, and laughter echoed off the buildings.

The plaza was lit by crisscrossing strings of Edison lights that zigzagged across the street like a canopy. They cast most of their light straight down, which meant we could still see glittering constellations of stars overhead. The moon was nearly full, and a few silvery clouds reflected its light in every direction. The flowerbeds were illuminated by solar lights at their base.

Sadie and I were dancing side by side. I was showing her one of my patented Marley moves—a twirling, lurching ballerina spin I still hadn't quite mastered—when a tall, dark, and handsome figure stepped out of the crowd and took me by the hand. With his assistance, I could complete the pirouette without falling over. When I came back full circle to see who had helped me, I was shocked to find myself face to face with Jack Edgewood.

He smiled, and without a word, we began to dance together. He guided me through a simple two-step, and I followed his lead as if we had been dancing together for years.

I marveled at his unexpected grace. There was a smoothness to his movements, a confidence that I hadn't expected. Dancing with him, I could feel the strength in his body—and his soul.

As the last notes of the song faded away, the small country-western group on the bandstand shifted gears. The lead singer, a man with a weathered hat that had seen its fair share of sunsets, gave a quick nod to his bandmates. The drummer gently eased into a softer rhythm, setting a more reflective pace. The guitarist strummed a series of chords that evoked the expansive night sky, while the bassist slowed his tempo, grounding the music in a deep, resonant foundation.

The fiddler, who until now had been providing lively, foot-stomping melodies, played longer, drawn-out notes, painting aural pictures of the wide-open spaces and starry skies. The violinist took up a haunting melody, weaving a tapestry of sound that felt as vast and deep as the night sky above. The drummer, who had kept everyone on their feet with rhythms that pulsed like the heart of the festival, now provided a soft, steady beat that mimicked the expectant heartbeat of the crowd.

Then, with a sudden burst of sound and light, the first fireworks rocketed into the night sky, marking the festival's grand finale.

The band launched into a soulful rendition of a classic country ballad, their music a perfect complement to the visual spectacle. Each explosion in the sky was mirrored by a crescendo in the music, creating a symphony of sight and sound that captivated everyone present. The band and the fireworks were in perfect sync, the music amplifying the beauty of the light show, and the brilliant cascades of colors lighting up the faces of everyone around us.

As the fireworks shot into the sky, exploding in a cascade of colors, the music raced toward a crescendo, the sound swelling in a perfect complement to the visual spectacle. Each burst of light was matched by a burst of sound, the music painting the night with its own form of magic. The melodies seemed to dance with the fireworks, each note a reflection of light, each chord a mirror to the joy and wonder of the moment.

I found myself standing beside Jack, Sadie, Eleanor, and Clara. Our hands were linked in a chain of camaraderie and shared experience, a tangible reminder of the journey we had embarked upon together.

In one spectacular burst that seemed to illuminate the air directly over our heads, Violet appeared, descending in an ethereal shower of glittering lights and stars to take her place among our little group.

Jack let out a low whistle of appreciation at a spectacular burst of light. Without thinking, he squeezed my hand.

The warmth of his touch, steady and grounding, sent an unexpected shiver down my spine. I glanced up at him, his face illuminated by flickering bursts of gold and blue. For a moment, he wasn't the enigmatic detective or the preternatural enforcer of rules—he was just Jack, watching the sky with quiet awe, standing beside me as if this night, this moment, was something worth holding onto.

Sadie, with her historian's soul, had tears of joy in her eyes, moved by the continuity of tradition and community spirit. Eleanor and Clara, the timeless guardians of Enchanted Springs' magical heritage, shared a look of quiet satisfaction, their faces alight with the fireworks' reflection.

As the final, cacophonous round of fireworks soared high and exploded in a shower of sparkling light, a collective gasp rose from the crowd. The band gently brought the song to a close, their last notes lingering in the air like the last traces of light, followed by a moment of awe-struck silence. Then, as if on cue, the square erupted in applause and cheers, a spontaneous celebration of the moment and all it represented.

In that instant, surrounded by the echoes of history and the promise of tomorrow, I realized how deeply I had become woven into the fabric of Enchanted Springs. This town, with its ghosts, its magic, and its endless capacity for wonder, had claimed a piece of my heart—and I didn't want to leave.

As the crowd dispersed, leaving behind the echoes of the day's joy, we remained a little longer, basking in the afterglow of the fireworks and the festival. The night was starry and clear, the air filled with the scent of summer and the faint hint of magic that always lingered in Enchanted Springs.

"Well, that's one for the history books. Another Founders Festival to remember." My grandmother's voice was soft, but it carried in the quiet square.

"Yes," I agreed, squeezing her hand. "And many more to come."

Chapter 48

Dawn of a New Day

THE ANTIQUE SHOP SMELLED of brewed coffee, aged wood, and a faint hint of lavender—a scent that had, somehow, become home. I curled my fingers around my coffee cup, letting the warmth sink in as I stared at my grandmother and Eleanor across the worn oak table. They were studying me like a pair of expert appraisers, as if determining my value, my purpose.

Eleanor, seated comfortably in one of the shop's high-backed chairs, sighed with the air of someone wrapping up a long and complex transaction. "Well, my dear, I suppose you've realized it by now."

I raised an eyebrow. "Realized what?"

Grandma Clara took a long sip of her coffee before setting the cup down with a decisive clink. "That you belong here, Marley."

The words hit differently than I expected. I'd known this was coming—I felt it in my bones—but hearing it spoken aloud made it real.

Eleanor reached across the table and patted my hand. "I'm not as spry as I used to be," she admitted. "Time travel takes a toll, I'm afraid. At long last, this shop is ready for a new caretaker. Someone who can bridge the past and the present."

She leaned in, lowering her voice as if sharing a great secret. "Someone like you."

"Gram did mention that you were thinking of retiring."

"Oh, in this business, we never really retire. Magic must carry on. But I'm not getting any younger, and I'd like you to take over. You're the right person to continue its legacy."

I felt torn. For one thing, I couldn't help but wonder about the practicalities. "But my life in Miami," I started. "My photography."

Gram nodded thoughtfully. "You'll never have to leave that behind. Your photography skills are an integral part of your magic."

She was right. Plus I could probably manage my corporate clients from anywhere with Internet access.

The idea of taking over the shop, of being a part of something so integral to the town's history, filled me with excitement. "I'd be honored," I said, still pondering the implications. "But if you're offering to sell me the shop, you should know that there's no way I can afford it."

"Oh, money's not the issue. I have a bill of sale right here for you, dear, and I think you'll find the terms agreeable."

She tottered over to the checkout counter and pulled out a single sheet of paper. It was simply a few lines of elegant calligraphy that, if I read it correctly, would convey the entire property to me, lock, stock, and barrel, for a dollar.

I inhaled. A dollar. There had to be a catch.

"Okay. I can afford that. But I don't know anything about antiques. I'd probably run the shop into the ground within just a few months."

"Not to worry," Eleanor said, smiling. "I'll help you settle in. Plus the position comes with a generous salary, as well as an endowment. Money is hardly a concern."

I looked at her quizzically. She reached over and took my hand in hers. "Guarding the portal isn't just a magical calling. There are practical considerations, too. So if some of us with knowledge of the timeline happen to put in a good word for an up-and-coming stock... well, we slide a few dollars into the account. Not enough to make or break the company as it gets established, but over time, our investments have been proven to be quite lucrative."

Sadie spoke up. I hadn't even seen her come in, but she was smiling. "Not to mention the reward."

"What reward?"

"When Colette disappeared, her husband Ricardo offered a five-hundred dollar reward for information that would lead to her return. Many people thought it was a cover for his own guilty conscience. He never rescinded the reward, though, even when he went home to Cuba. The money was invested in the S&P 500, with the city as trustee."

Sadie grinned. "Do you know what that means?"

I shook my head.

Jack answered. I hadn't seen him come in, either. "Today, that reward is worth about three million dollars. And since there were no conditions on the reward, like Colette's safe return, the city's attorneys agree that you and Sadie are the legal recipients."

As if on cue, Ivy walked into the shop, carrying a manilla folder.

"Sorry I'm late, everyone. I just wanted to do one last check of the records before I came over."

She took a seat at the table. "After you called, I did some research. Did you know that Eleanor Somerville has owned the Enchanted Antique Shop for almost fifty years? Pardon me for saying so, Eleanor, but you don't look old enough to have been in business for five decades."

Eleanor sat up a little straighter in her chair and fluffed her hair. "I'm a firm believer in Noxzema and beauty rest."

Ivy nodded. "You're a wise woman.."

She looked back down at her paperwork. "Well, what's really incredible is that I went back through the county's property records, and the previous owner had the property for fifty years, too!"

She turned to me for a response. I turned to Eleanor, who merely smiled.

Ivy continued. "But here's the really strange thing. In all the time since it was built, the Mercantile, and now the antique shop, has never been on the market. Every fifty years, it simply changes hands, and always for a dollar."

She read through the bill of sale, then passed me an updated contract, along with the abstract of title.

"It's just as straightforward as it looks," she said. "I see arrangements like this every so often. While the purchase price is low, the agreement itself is rock solid and contractually sound. Honestly, if I were you, I'd snap it up."

"But would I be obligated to run the shop for the next fifty years?"

She laughed. "Only time will tell, Marley."

I looked down at the bill of sale Eleanor had handed me. A single dollar, a stroke of a pen, and I would own the Enchanted Antique Shop. Not to mention the very generous signing bonus, courtesy of Ricardo Rios.

My mind reeled at the thought of it—the lives that had passed through this place, the caretakers who had guarded its magic, the secrets it held, the mysteries still waiting to be uncovered. I wasn't just taking over a business. I was stepping into something much larger than myself. A legacy. A destiny.

I signed the contract, sealing my new role with the flourish of a pen. In a moment of perfect timing, Gram's assistant Kate appeared, bearing a silver platter laden with an assortment of baked delicacies. Sadie broke out a bottle of chilled champagne, which we sipped from antique crystal flutes, with hand-cut facets that cast rainbow prisms around the room. Then Ivy took the paperwork back to her office to file.

At Violet's request, the soft strains of jazz played from the gramophone, and she treated us to an impromptu dance. But, of course, Violet being Violet, she couldn't leave it at just a simple twirl. She began to dance in mid-air, high-kicking the Charleston, just as she had done in the fountain when I first got to town.

Eleanor sighed. "We should have expected this."

"Just let her have it," Gram murmured, sipping her champagne.

Violet spun, dipped, and flipped herself into the air with im-possible grace, her form shimmering with ghostly radiance. When she landed her final flourish—a dazzling high kick—the entire room burst into applause.

She curtsied, glowing with satisfaction. "And that, ladies and gentlemen, is how you mark the end of one era, and the start of a new Golden Age."

Twila leaped into my lap, her spectral form warm despite her incorporeal nature. She blinked up at me, her eerie, ever-chang-ing eyes swirling with new colors—not just blue, green, or vio-let this time, but shades I couldn't name, like a Miami sunset.

I scratched behind her ears, and a soft purring vibration filled the room—not just a sound, but a hum of magic that tickled the air. The lights flickered, the gramophone's song warped for a second, and every single antique clock in the shop ticked in perfect unison.

A final confirmation.

I wasn't just accepting a new job. The magic of the Enchanted Antique Shop had accepted me.

Chapter 49

About the Author

CIELLE KENNER'S BOOKS ARE set in the small town of Enchanted Springs—where ghosts are friendly, magic is real, and time is anything but linear. It's a charming small town in Central Florida, loosely based on Cielle's own real-life hometown near Ponce de Leon's legendary Fountain of Youth.

Cielle started writing professionally at the age of seventeen, first as a newspaper reporter, then as a magazine editor and author of several non-fiction books. Along the way, she earned a bachelor's degree in philosophy from California State University.

Cielle is a certified tarot master and certified astrologer, and an expert in ancient mythology and storytelling models like the Hero's Journey. She's also a graduate of the Citizens Police Academy, and her formal training in police procedures and criminal investigations imbues her mystery stories with a sense of realism and authenticity.

When she's not writing, Cielle finds inspiration in red wine, baked potatoes, and gently haunted antique shops. She likes cats and dogs equally; at the moment, she's dog mom to a feisty Jack Russell terrier named Dottie. Cielle also likes to crochet, even though she's not very good at it, and she has more yarn hidden in her craft closet than she'll ever be able to use.

Cielle is available for book signings, book talks, and book club discussions. You can find her online at ciellekenner.com, and across social media @ciellekenner.